"So You're Afraid of Yourself," He Mocked.

But she wouldn't let him kiss her. "Not again!" she cried. "Never again!"

"Is that a challenge?" He took a step toward her and Nicola found she was pressed against the wall.

"Of course it isn't," she protested. But he had noted her nervousness and his eyes glinted in triumph. Nicola felt his sheer animal magnetism threatening to overcome her senses. She tried to summon the willpower to walk away in cold disdain, but she was powerless to move.

And then she was in his arms and it was herself she was fighting, doing battle against her own treacherous instinct to yield. . . .

Dear Reader:

Silhouette Romances is an exciting new publishing venture. We will be presenting the very finest writers of contemporary romantic fiction as well as outstanding new talent in this field. It is our hope that our stories, our heroes and our heroines will give you, the reader, all you want from romantic fiction.

Also, *you* play an important part in our future plans for Silhouette Romances. We welcome any suggestions or comments on our books and I invite you to write to us at the address below.

So, enjoy this book and all the wonderful romances from Silhouette. They're for *you!*

Karen Solem
Editor-in-Chief
Silhouette Books
P.O. Box 769
New York, N.Y. 10019

NANCY JOHN
Outback Summer

Silhouette Romance

Published by Silhouette Books New York

America's Publisher of Contemporary Romance

Other Silhouette Romances by Nancy John

Tormenting Flame
The Spanish House
To Trust Tomorrow

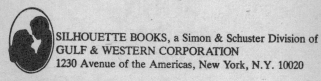

SILHOUETTE BOOKS, a Simon & Schuster Division of
GULF & WESTERN CORPORATION
1230 Avenue of the Americas, New York, N.Y. 10020

Copyright © 1981 by Nancy John

Distributed by Pocket Books

ISBN: 0-671-57085-4

First Silhouette printing June, 1981

10 9 8 7 6 5 4 3 2 1

All of the characters in this book are fictitious. Any resemblance to actual persons, living or dead, is purely coincidental.

Map copyright by Tony Ferrara

America's Publisher of Contemporary Romance

Printed in the U.S.A.

Chapter One

Through the windows of the small plane carrying her from Sydney, Nicola looked down at the parched brown landscape below, so very different from the lush green English countryside she had left only a couple of days ago. Here and there, a line of trees traced the meandering course of a dried-up creek; hardly ever did she see the glint of water. It had been a long "dry" this summer, everyone on the plane was telling her.

Some time back they had passed over the Blue Mountains, and already they had touched down at a number of small townships to discharge a passenger or two and unload mailbags and parcels of freight. The very next landing would be her stopoff, Boolaroo, where her friend Angie would be waiting to meet her. As the little oasis of tree-encircled dwellings came into view and the plane banked for its run in, Nicola felt her excitement rising at the prospect of the wonderful holiday she was going to have over the next two months.

Five minutes later, her suitcase and holdall at her feet, she stood gazing around her at the huddle of airport buildings, wishing that she was wearing something cooler than her navy blazer suit in this relentlessly scorching heat. She ran a hand through her dark curly hair, easing it away from the nape of her neck.

A grizzle-headed man, wearing a peaked khaki cap, ambled toward her.

"Hey, you must be Miss Wyatt, right?"

"Yes, that's right." Nicola smiled at him nervously. "I was expecting to be met here, but there doesn't seem to be anyone. . . ."

"Nope, that's what I've got to tell you about. We had a call from Angie Carson out at Dandaraga to say that their transport's conked out again, so they can't come fetch you."

"Oh, no!" Nicola exclaimed in dismay. Behind her, the plane was already revving up to take off for its next destination, so it meant that she was being left stranded here in this sun-baked wilderness. She already knew from Angie that the Carson homestead lay more than a hundred miles from this small bush township, with nothing in between but a few other sheep stations.

"What am I supposed to do?" she asked unhappily. "Can I get a taxi? Hire a car?"

"No chance! But not to worry, love; they'll be here for you sometime tomorrow."

"Tomorrow?" she gasped.

"Yep. Angie said to take a room at the hotel, and they'll settle the bill." He jerked his thumb over his shoulder, indicating a single-story clapboard building some one hundred yards away. White lettering on its corrugated-iron roof announced it to be the Commercial Hotel.

Nicola's spirits took a dive. The thought of spending a night here was a terrible anticlimax after having jetted halfway around the world, with only the briefest pause at Sydney to change from the huge jetliner to the light plane of the Australian internal airways. Despite her excitement, she was feeling more than a little weary and travel-stained. She had been longing to see Angie's cheerful smiling face and be whisked off to the Carson homestead, where she would be able to enjoy a leisurely shower and change into something cooler, to relax in friendly company.

The man gave a sudden exclamation. "Say, I've got

an idea. See that bloke over there? He's going within a kangaroo's jump of Dandaraga, and he can drop you off on his way."

Nicola felt a flood of relief. "Are you sure he wouldn't mind?"

"If I know that fella, he'll leap at the chance—too right he will! How many beaut sheilas with gorgeous big brown eyes do you think we get around here? I'll just go over and lay it on for you."

"Beaut sheilas," Nicola supposed, were beautiful girls. They certainly talked differently here! But no doubt after a few weeks at Dandaraga station she would sound just the same. She dropped the subject and turned to watch her new acquaintance walk off to intercede on her behalf.

The man to whom he had referred, clad in khaki cotton drill trousers and a checked shirt with the sleeves rolled up, was humping two heavy crates that had been unloaded from the plane into a dusty Range-Rover. He had his back to Nicola, but she could see that he was very tall and big-boned. He wore no hat and his fair hair was bleached by the sun, whereas his neck and bare arms were burned almost to the color of mahogany. When the airport man went up and spoke to him, he swung around to look in Nicola's direction. Thumbs hitched into his wide leather belt, he stood and gave her a slow, cool appraisal. She could feel his eyes traveling over her, registering every curve of her slender body and the slim length of her legs. It was almost, Nicola thought with a flash of irritation, as though she were a horse he was thinking of buying.

Apparently satisfied with what he could see, he came strolling over to her with long, leisurely strides. He was incredibly good-looking, she had to admit, in that rugged, craggy-featured way that appealed to a great many women. And it was all too obvious that he knew it. There was a haughty aloofness in his lean, angular face that suggested supreme self-confidence. He had a firm mouth, a straight nose, high cheekbones, and a strong chin divided by a deep cleft. Sun wrinkles radiated from the corners of his intensely blue eyes, which at the moment were narrowed against the dazzling glare.

"I hear you want a lift," he drawled.

"If it won't inconvenience you too much," Nicola replied, with a hint of sarcasm. She didn't at all care for the idea of being beholden to this man.

"As it happens," he clipped, "it won't inconvenience me. But even if it would, I'd feel obliged to give you a ride to the Carsons' place. Here in the outback, pommie girl, we have to try to help each other. So let's get your gear aboard and we'll be on our way."

Belatedly, Nicola felt sudden qualms at the thought of setting off on a hundred-mile drive into lonely bush country with a complete stranger. Her apprehension must have been apparent on her face, for he gave a curt laugh and said sardonically, "Guess the young lady thinks I might take advantage of her on the way, Banjo. You'd better reassure her that she'll be safe with me."

"Not so sure I can at that, you young sinner!" replied Banjo, grinning widely. Then, giving Nicola a friendly wink, he added, "You'll be okay, love; he's a well-respected identity in these parts."

It was as simple as that. Within a couple of minutes her luggage had been dumped with the crates in the back of the Range-Rover and Nicola was seated in the passenger seat beside the driver. Then, with a thrust of power, they were off, leaving a cloud of red dust hanging in the hot still air behind them.

They drove through the main street of the little settlement where there were trim weatherboard bungalows, a few shops, a post office, and a garage. Then they crossed a bridge over an almost dried-up creek overhung with drooping trees that Nicola couldn't identify. Some magnificently colored birds were wading in the muddy pools, and she was fascinated to see on a telegraph wire dozens of tiny green budgerigars, looking like bright jewels strung along a necklace. As they left the township behind and set off along a dusty dirt road, Nicola kept glancing around her, eager to miss nothing—though there wasn't much to be seen in this flat, almost barren landscape, except for a few sheep grazing among the coarse tufts of tawny grass and scrubby bushes. Then suddenly she gave a cry of delight as she spotted a kangaroo. Startled from its feeding by their approach, it went bounding off into a clump of spindly trees, giving gigantic leaps powered by its powerful hind legs, its forepaws dangling in front of its chest.

The man beside her laughed. "You haven't seen a 'roo before?"

"Only in the London zoo," she told him. "It's incredible, isn't it, the way they can jump so far?"

"Anything up to thirty feet," he informed her. "And they can travel at thirty miles an hour, too—though that's only for short distances to get themselves out of danger." After a little pause, he added with amusement, "You seem as excited about it as if you were a small girl."

Flushing a little, Nicola said defensively, "Well, it *is* exciting for me. I've always wanted to see the Australian outback, and this is like a dream come true. So why should I pretend otherwise?"

"Too right, why should you?"

A swing gate barred the road ahead, and he pulled up and sprang down to open it; then, after driving through, he got out again and closed it carefully before driving on. When, a few minutes later, they came to another gate, Nicola suggested, "Look, wouldn't it be more sensible for me to get out and open it while you drive straight on through?"

"If you're sure that's okay by you," he said, and Nicola felt warmed by his smile of appreciation.

When she climbed back in again, the gate closed, she

11

said, "It's really very good of you to give me this lift, Mr. . . ."

"Forget the thanks," he said dismissively. "I take it that you're a friend of the Carsons'?"

"Well, yes—of Angie's, actually. We met when she was in England last year. I was at agricultural college and she was working as an *au pair* for the family I lodged with. We got friendly, and at the end of term we spent a vacation together going around the tourist spots that Angie wanted to see. Most of all she was crazy about London. She thought it was fantastic after the loneliness of the outback here."

"The outback doesn't have to be lonely," he retorted. Flicking her a swift glance, he went on meaningfully, "It all depends on the company that's available and what you make of your opportunities."

Nicola said nothing and stared straight ahead through the windshield. She was hoping fervently that Banjo's reassurance had been sincere and that this man was to be trusted. Now that they had left the few habitations around the airstrip behind, as far as she could see in every direction there was just a wide-open expanse of emptiness.

After driving for a few minutes in silence, he said, "So now you're paying your friend Angie a visit? Will you be over here for Christmas?"

"Yes. I'm staying till the end of January. Then Angie and I are having a week in Sydney together before I fly back to England. I must say, it seems awfully strange the way your seasons are all switched around. The thought of Christmas in summer . . ." Her voice trailed off in amazement.

"Quite a time for you to be away from home," he commented dryly. "How will your parents like eating their Christmas turkey and plum pudding without you? To say nothing of your boyfriend."

"I haven't any parents," Nicola explained. "My father died when I was ten, and then my mother passed away two years ago."

"That's tough." There was another long pause, then: "You only answered half my question, though."

"What do you mean?"

"About your boyfriend. How does he like the prospect of being separated from you for so long?"

"I haven't got a boyfriend, not in that sense. Er . . . what I mean is, there's nobody special."

He gave a scornful exclamation. "Those pommie males must be a feeble lot if they let a delectable sheila like you escape them."

His tone put Nicola on the defensive again, despite the implied compliment. "I've only come away for a couple of months," she reminded him.

"Don't be so sure," he replied enigmatically as he swung the Range-Rover over the rutted bottom of a dried-up gully. He was driving with one bronzed hand on the steering wheel, his other elbow resting on the side of the vehicle. "Do you come from farming stock, then, going to agricultural college?" he asked after a moment.

"Oh, no! I was born in the city . . . Bristol, actually. But Mum always maintained that I was a country girl at heart. It was always my ambition to go in for some kind of farming."

"And now you've got all the qualifications?"

"Well, I wouldn't exactly claim that," she said nervously, conscious of the underlying mockery in his tone. "I got my diploma last year, and since then I've been doing practical work on various farms in the south of England."

"With sheep?" he queried sharply.

"Well, yes, sometimes. On the last farm I was at they had about fifty ewes."

"Fifty!" he echoed with a scornful laugh. "Over here we count sheep by the thousand."

"I haven't noticed many around, though," she retorted, stung by his manner.

"Maybe not. But that's because in the outback we have to reckon in acres to the sheep rather than sheep to the acre. There are none of your cozy little English-style farms in these parts, with lush-growing grass for pasturage. Even the Carsons' place, a small one by our standards, covers something over four thousand acres. Not that Tony utilizes his land properly. He runs less than a thousand head of sheep—and even from those few, he got a poor-quality clip at the shearing a couple of months back."

"You seem to know a lot about Angie's brother," she said, making it a reproof.

"Naturally I do. He's my next-door neighbor, even though the homesteads are a good thirty miles apart."

Nicola felt a cold shiver run down her spine. The Carsons' next-door neighbor . . . Why hadn't she thought of that possibility before? She knew now that her niggle of anxiety about accepting the lift, which she'd airily dismissed as quite irrational, had in reality been a shrewd judgment on her part. But it had never occurred to her that this man, dressed so casually in cotton drill trousers and a rumpled shirt, humping heavy crates into the back of a Range-Rover, could be the owner of one of the largest sheep stations in this part of New South Wales. And yet, hadn't she been stupid not to realize that someone with his arrogant self-confidence hardly fitted the image of the stockman or foreman that she'd taken him to be?

"You . . . you never told me your name," she said faintly.

"Didn't I? It's Rossiter. Garth Rossiter."

Even though Nicola was quite prepared for this now, she still couldn't avoid flinching away from him in her seat. Her reaction didn't escape him, and he shot her a swift sideways glance.

"I see that you've been well primed about me! What kind of ugly picture did Angie Carson paint, I wonder, to make you nearly jump out of your skin like that?"

Nicola wouldn't have dared to repeat most of the things her friend had said about the man. So she replied with a shrug, "Angie just happened to mention that you and her brother don't see eye to eye about . . . about this and that."

Garth Rossiter laughed shortly. "You mean he doesn't see eye to eye with me!"

"Isn't that a very self-centered way of looking at a situation?" she inquired coldly. "Why *should* Tony Carson be forced to sell out to you? You're talking about land which was farmed by his father, and his grandfather before that. Just because you happen to be rich and powerful, it doesn't automatically give you the right—"

"If I happen to be rich and powerful," he interrupted, "it's because I've worked hard to get where I am. I don't spend day after day just whining about my bad luck and doing nothing to rectify things."

"Are you suggesting that Tony *does?*"

"Too right I am! I'm suggesting that he thinks an extra-long drought is his personal misfortune, and not just a trick of climate common to all sheep farmers— something that has to be battled with. I'm suggesting that Tony Carson thinks a drop in wool prices on the commodity market is a problem suffered by him alone, and not a situation to be weathered until things pick up again."

"It's easy for *you* to talk," Nicola protested defensively. "I don't suppose a man like you has ever known what it's like to be really hard up, and constantly pressed by the bank manager to clear your overdraft . . ." She broke off, realizing how indiscreet it was of her to speak about Angie's brother's financial problems—though no doubt Garth Rossiter knew all there was to be known on that score.

A silence fell between them, a hostile, brooding silence that grew more and more uncomfortable as it lengthened. Garth pressed his foot down on the gas pedal and their speed mounted until the Range-Rover was bouncing wildly on the rutted track. *He* might be used to traveling like this, Nicola thought furiously, but *she* wasn't. Even by clutching the door for support it was all she could do to keep in her seat. She had half a mind to insist that he stop at once and let her get out. But that would mean being stranded under this pitiless sun, perhaps for hours. Since leaving the airstrip, she realized despairingly, they hadn't passed a single vehicle of any kind.

Well, if there was no question of getting out, neither was she going to beg him to slow down. Let him prove that he was an unmannered boor by making the journey horribly uncomfortable for her! She refused to utter a single murmur of protest.

When Angie had been in England she had often referred to their wealthy neighbor, Garth Rossiter, who herded some forty thousand head of sheep on an estate that measured over thirty-five miles across at its widest point. There had been a tinge of envy in her friend's voice as she spoke, and, knowing that the man was unmarried, Nicola had once teased Angie about having her eye on him.

"Not me, thank you very much," Angie had snorted in derision. "Garth may be as rich as any girl could wish for, and dead sexy with it, but I'm not looking for a husband who farms sheep. Give me a Sydneysider any time, and a nice little house in the suburbs . . . that would suit me just fine."

In the letters Angie had written since her return home, she had become increasingly bitter about Garth Rossiter. It seemed that he was taking advantage of her brother's cash-flow problems to try and force him to sell out.

The wretched man is determined on making life difficult for poor Tony in every way he can. Just recently he had the nerve to sink a new borehole right up against our boundary fence to get at underground water that by rights should be ours.

*Now, if you please, he's piping some of it back in
our direction and making out that he's being
generous. Honestly, it's the limit! The land on the
other side of us is another big sheep station owned
by a man named Howard Drysdale, who just has
the one daughter. So Garth reckons that if he can
buy us out he'd have a common boundary with the
Drysdale place. Then all he'd have to do is marry
Zoe Drysdale and he'd be all set to take control of
the whole kit and kaboodle. That would double
Garth's acreage, Tony says, and make him just
about the biggest sheep farmer in the whole of New
South Wales. It's a well-known fact that old man
Drysdale is thinking about retiring, and what more
natural than to hand his land over to his son-in-
law?*

In Angie's next letter she had written about an
incident when a large number of Tony's sheep had
escaped onto Garth Rossiter's land.

*He claims to have returned every one of them to
us, but Tony is positive that's not true. And
anyway, Tony wants to know, how come the fence
got broken in the first place? He says there was no
sign of the posts being loose when he last checked.*

Remembering all that, reflecting on what a ruthless,
calculating man Garth Rossiter was, Nicola saw no
reason why she should put herself out to thaw the
freezing atmosphere that had developed between them,
and for his part he seemed equally ready to remain
silent for the rest of the journey. Every now and then
he pulled up sharply before a gate, and, without saying
a word, Nicola got down to hold it open while he drove
through. Then once, instead of waiting for her to climb
back in after closing the gate, he switched off the
engine and climbed out, too.

"What's wrong?" she demanded.

"Nothing's wrong," he said dourly. "I wanted to show you something. This way."

With a shrug of resignation, Nicola followed him as he strode off briskly in the direction of a rise of land that climbed to a ridge with an outcrop of broken rocks. She had a curious feeling of unreality, born, she supposed, of the scorching heat and the surrounding silence, the great cloudless vault of blue sky and the deep indigo shadows cast by every boulder, every scrubby tree and bush—and the dominating presence of this arrogantly good-looking man who had such a potent aura of masculinity about him.

He strode on, and Nicola had quite a job keeping up with him, until they had crested the rise. There he stopped and stood with his hands on his hips, gazing out across the undulating landscape to the distant vistas. Nicola caught her breath in awe at the strange stark beauty of this never-ending land that stretched before them, on and on until it was swallowed up by the lilac mists of distance. All the colors were soft and muted, and there was a subtle but distinctive aromatic smell— of grass, and the dusty earth; of eucalyptus from the gum trees, and other fragrances she couldn't begin to identify. And in all this immensity, it seemed to her eye, nothing moved. There was just silence and still-ness.

"That's the Australian outback for you," said Garth Rossiter abruptly. "What do you think of it, pommie girl?"

"It . . . it's beautiful," Nicola whispered, a lump in her throat.

"You think so? Most people who come here consider it harsh, forbidding country—especially when there's been a long dry like now."

"Oh, no, I still think it's beautiful," she insisted. "There's something . . . well, magnificently primitive about it. Magical! I can't quite explain what I mean."

Garth nodded, as if he understood and approved.

"You see the slight dip way over there in the distance," he said, lifting his long arm to point. "It's a shallow valley, really, of course. That's Dandaraga, the Carsons' place."

Nicola shielded her eyes against the brassy, searing sunlight. "It looks greener than the rest."

"It is . . . a favored spot. The best parcel of land in a devil of a lot of territory."

"Is that why you want it so badly?" she said before she could stop herself.

"My land," Garth went on, as if she hadn't spoken, "starts at that outcrop of red rock over there to the right. It stretches as far as you can see, and beyond."

Nicola couldn't hold back the bitter words. "And yet you still want more?"

"When I inherited Kuranda station from my father nine years ago, at the age of twenty-four," he said slowly, "it comprised only a tenth of what I now own."

"Which means that you've trampled on other, less fortunate people to add to your empire," she flung at him furiously. "Just as now you're trying to trample on Tony."

Garth Rossiter gave her a dangerous look. "I've been successful in making the land pay under modern conditions, where others have failed."

"Bully for you!" she remarked scathingly. "Only there's no point in your boasting to me, Mr. Rossiter. I'm not one bit impressed!"

With that Nicola turned and made to walk back to the Range-Rover fifty yards below them. But before she could take the first step a hand with fingers of steel clamped around her arm and she was forcibly swung back to face him. She expected the angry lash of his tongue, but there was merely a look of amusement on his lean features.

"Guess I'll have to find another way to impress you, pommie girl," he said mockingly.

"What . . . what do you mean?"

He made no reply but just stood looking down at her, his eyes seeming to burn into her very soul. With only inches separating them, Nicola was tinglingly conscious of his virile strength, the animal heat of his body.

"Please!" she said faintly. "You're hurting. Let me go!"

But instead he swiftly bent his head and put his lips against hers. It was no more than a feather-light pressure, and all over in an instant, yet Nicola was electrified, stunned. Her heart seemed to stop beating entirely, then began to pound again with fierce hammer blows. She found that she was trembling in every limb. It was from anger, of course . . . anger that he should dare to take such a liberty.

"I suppose you think that was clever," she raged. "Getting me here in the middle of nowhere, and . . . and forcibly kissing me."

"You call that a kiss?" he remarked scornfully. "Where have you been all your life, little girl," he mocked, "if you count a gentle little peck like that as a kiss?"

She didn't intend to stand there bandying words with him. With all the dignity she could muster, she said in a strangled voice, "Will you kindly let me go, Mr. Rossiter?"

"Is that what you really want?" he countered. "And before you answer that question, I may as well tell you that if you say 'Yes, it is,' I shan't believe you."

Nicola began to make a furious answer when she was arrested by the sound of an engine. Glancing around, she saw a motorbike approaching in a cloud of dust. If she could catch the rider's attention, Garth Rossiter would be forced to let her go.

The motorbike came roaring along the last stretch of road and slowed beside the Range-Rover. Garth gave the rider a wave and got a cheerful thumbs-up sign in return as the man dismounted to open the gate.

This was her chance, Nicola thought; she had only to struggle and it would be apparent that she was being held against her will. Yet for some unaccountable reason she remained motionless, and the next instant her opportunity was gone. The motorbike's engine revved and it was off with a roar that soon diminished to a drone in the far distance.

"You didn't shout for help, I notice," Garth observed ironically.

Raging inwardly against herself, Nicola replied through tight lips, "Would it have done any good? I have no doubt that he's a friend of yours."

Garth nodded. "Jeff Anstey, my station manager. He and his wife, Mary, have a bungalow near the homestead at Kuranda, so you'll be meeting them when you come over."

"I very much doubt if I shall have any cause to visit your homestead," said Nicola frostily.

He grinned down at her. "Oh, but you will, pommie girl! You'll soon discover that here in the outback you have to take what company there is. People are so thin on the ground that you can't afford to be choosy. Not that meeting Jeff will be any hardship. He's a really nice fellow—one of nature's gentlemen."

"It's a pity the same can't be said about his employer," Nicola retorted. "No one could apply such a description to you."

"Granted," he said, with a twist of his lips. "But as to that being a pity, I'm not so sure that it matters. From what I've seen of you, I expect that you're a warm-blooded girl who would readily respond to a really virile man—and not care whether he's a gentleman or not!"

"Well, you're wrong," she threw back furiously. "Utterly wrong."

"I wonder if I am," he drawled. "Let's put it to the test, shall we?"

"For heaven's sake," Nicola protested hotly. "I'm

not in the mood for playing silly games." She wished desperately now that she hadn't let the man on the motorbike go by.

"Who said anything about playing games?" he quipped. "What I had in mind was in the nature of a serious scientific experiment. The aim is to prove once and for all that Nicola Wyatt is not the prim, wishy-washy little English miss she pretends to be."

"If you dare try to kiss me again," she stormed, "I'll . . . I'll . . ."

"What will you do?" he taunted, his blue eyes turning to glittering stones.

What *could* she do? "You . . . you'll make me despise you," she responded weakly.

"But you despise me already, don't you?" he jeered. "So I might just as well be hung for a sheep as for a lamb, as the saying so aptly goes."

In an instant his arms were locked around her in a tight embrace, and as Nicola tried desperately to pull away she found herself crushed against his lean, hard body. Relentlessly his lips claimed hers, taking possession of her mouth in a fiercely passionate kiss. With a moan of resignation she closed her eyes, feeling herself drowning in a great tidal wave of sensual excitement such as she had never experienced before.

They stood locked together for long moments that seemed to stretch to all eternity, and Nicola felt lightheaded with the wild ecstasy that surged through her veins. Her body became pliant, her softness molding ever more intimately to his muscled hardness as she felt her own stirrings of desire in response to his mounting passion.

When at last the kiss came to an end, she released a long shivering sigh of pleasure that rippled through her whole being. Garth's steel-strong arms immediately loosed their grip, and he gave a low laugh.

"The experiment was a hundred percent successful," he declared, his voice slightly shaky. "A most gratifying demonstration that I was right in my judgment of you."

Despite the sun's burning heat, Nicola flinched as if he had doused her with ice-cold water. Her fists came up and pressed against the solid wall of his chest, thrusting her back from him.

"You . . . you're hateful!" she spat out.

"Yet you find me intensely attractive," he drawled. "Interesting paradox, isn't it?"

"If you think for one moment . . ." Nicola struggled to find the right words, words that would pierce his armor of conceit. "If you seriously imagine that I feel anything for you except loathing and detestation, you couldn't be more wrong. You're nothing but an arrogant pig."

"Fighting talk!" he observed unconcernedly. "Only you'd better remember, pommie girl, that you're all alone with me in wild bush country." When he made a slight movement Nicola backed away instinctively, at which his mouth curved in a laugh of cruel amusement. "Still jumpy? Ah, well, I don't blame you. With a passionate nature like yours you have to watch yourself, or things could get really out of hand."

"I'd be obliged," she said scathingly, "if you'd kindly keep such crude remarks to yourself, Mr. Rossiter."

"You prefer actions to words, do you?" he gibed. For a horrified moment Nicola was afraid that he was going to kiss her again, but instead he swung around and started to head down toward the waiting Range-Rover. "Come on, we'd better get moving. That is, if you feel you can trust yourself driving with me."

"It's you I can't trust, Mr. Rossiter," she retorted loftily. "I'd rather walk the rest of the way, thank you."

"Would you, now?" he mocked. "Then you must be a great deal tougher than anyone could possibly expect a girl with such a petite figure as yours to be."

"What's that supposed to mean?" she demanded, trying to conceal her anxiety. "It can't be far to walk now."

"Distances are deceptive in open country like this. It's a good ten miles of dusty track to Dandaraga, and in this sort of heat it would take every last ounce of your strength."

Nicola did not even try to hide her contempt. "You find it very amusing, don't you, that I have no alternative but to go with you?"

"I wouldn't exactly say amusing," he countered. "Interesting, rather. Girls—especially attractive ones—are a scarce commodity hereabouts, you know."

"I've no doubt you make sure that you don't go short of female company," she muttered, and instantly regretted that quick tongue of hers. Her gibe failed miserably, because he seemed to take it as a compliment.

"Too right; I don't allow myself to go short," he agreed, with a maddening smile of derision. "But that's not to say an addition to the fold isn't welcome. It's always nice to have an extra option."

This time Nicola somehow managed to restrain herself from hitting back at him and maintained her silence. By now they'd reached the Range-Rover, and she scrambled in quickly before Garth could attempt to give her a helping hand.

They drove off and Garth settled for a slower pace than hitherto, which was a great relief, as it meant she wasn't bumped around so much. It was also a relief that he made no further attempt at conversation. She sat gazing straight ahead, trying unsuccessfully to blot from her mind the awareness of this disturbing man beside her, his shoulder and thigh only inches from hers. Now and then, when he used the gearshift, his sunburned hand came directly within her field of vision, and she had an insane desire to reach out and touch the long, sinewy fingers. She forced herself to turn her head and look the other way, searching the scrubby pastures for grazing sheep.

Fifteen minutes later Garth drew up by a rickety gate with a sign in roughly painted letters, *Dandaraga*.

There was a mailbox nailed to an upright of the wire and pole fencing. The house wasn't visible, but Nicola guessed it must be in the grove of parched-looking trees just below them on the down-sloping track.

"Oh, good, we've arrived!" she exclaimed, not hiding the relief in her voice.

"Not yet!" said Garth laconically. "You still have the pleasure of my company for a little longer."

When Nicola had opened and shut the gate they resumed their journey, lurching down a rough track that followed the course of a little creek for another mile or so until at last a small group of buildings came into sight. The house, surrounded by a patch of fenced-off garden, was a single-storied board structure with a pitched roof, and a wire-screened veranda ran all along the front. At either end stood a large galvanized iron tank, which she guessed must be for storing water, and a small steel windmill revolved slowly in the hot air. It was only as they drew close that Nicola saw obvious signs of neglect and dilapidation. The cream-colored paintwork was cracked and peeling in places, and several of the boards had slipped out of place.

Without switching off the engine, Garth got out and unloaded her luggage, dumping it on the veranda steps. "Well, I'll be off now," he announced, turning back to the Range-Rover.

"But there doesn't seem to be anyone at home," Nicola said uneasily.

"You'll find the door open," he told her and leaped back into the driver's seat. "Be seeing you."

She looked at him unhappily, swallowing down the lump in her throat. "I've got to say thank you, at least, for bringing me here, Mr. Rossiter."

"Don't mention it. I told you, it's a rule of the outback to lend a helping hand whenever possible. Anyway, it was a real pleasure . . . for me! And by the way, another rule of the outback is not to stand on ceremony, so you'd better call me Garth. Cheerio, Nicola!"

As the Range-Rover swung in a tight U-turn and headed back along the track, disappearing into the scrubby trees, Nicola felt curiously lonely. She stood listening to the sound of the engine until it faded away to nothing. Somewhere nearby an unseen sheep bleated plaintively, and a bird in a tree overhead gave a sudden raucous call that had the sound of mocking laughter.

Chapter Two

"You must be Nicola . . . ?"

The voice, slightly querulous, made Nicola swing around to see a thin, middle-aged woman standing at the open screen door of the veranda. She wore a long cotton dressing robe, and her frizzy graying hair looked rather disheveled.

"That's right." Nicola walked over to her. "I suppose you're Angie's Aunt Janet?"

The woman nodded and pushed her gold-rimmed spectacles farther up her nose. "I couldn't come out before, dressed like this—not when I saw who was bringing you. I was having a nap," she went on by way of explanation. "I need to in the afternoons, in my present state of health."

"Oh, yes, I see," said Nicola, and added politely, "I'm sorry to hear that you're not well, Mrs. King."

She received a curt grunt in response. "You'd best bring your luggage in."

Humping the heavy suitcase and holdall, Nicola followed the woman into the house and across a square hallway decorated with potted ferns. "Angie and her brother are out, I suppose?" she ventured.

"In the paddocks. Where else, this time of day? Didn't you get the message that they couldn't come to collect you?"

"Yes, I did. I was going to take a room at the hotel,

as Angie suggested, but then a man at the airstrip, Banjo something-or-other, asked Mr. Rossiter to offer me a lift."

"Him!" The contempt was very expressive. "Always poking his nose in. I'm surprised you accepted."

"Well, I could hardly refuse," Nicola protested.

"I don't see why not. It isn't every girl who would choose to spend a couple of hours driving in the bush with a total stranger. Did Garth Rossiter try anything with you? A kiss, maybe? I wouldn't put it past him."

Nicola's face flamed scarlet, and she said defensively, "He was hardly a stranger, Mrs. King. I . . . I mean, I knew that he was a neighbor of yours, and the man at the airport vouched for him."

"Did he, now? I suppose Banjo Paterson thought it was real funny, sending you with *him.*" She gave Nicola a glare from behind her spectacles. "Angie must have told you about Garth Rossiter and how he does nothing but make trouble for us."

"Yes, she did. But I didn't realize who he was when we started out."

Janet King gave a grunt of disgust. "You mean to say you took a lift from a man without bothering to find out who he was? No wonder you young girls get into trouble!"

Nicola felt mortified that her visit to Dandaraga should have started off so badly.

"Oh, well, there's no harm done." she said, in an effort to make peace.

"No harm done?" the older woman echoed. "I wonder!"

That was something Nicola wondered, too. It had been an easy enough thing to say, but would anything ever be the same for her again after the devastating experience of being kissed by Garth Rossiter? She felt the color storming to her cheeks again as she relived the sensation of his lips on hers and the vibrant heat of his lean, hard body pressed so intimately against her own.

To try to cover her embarrassment, she stammered, "Perhaps I could go to my room now and clean myself up. I feel rather hot and sticky."

Janet King seemed to relent and gave a thin smile of apology. "Yes, of course, dear, you must be. And I'll make a pot of tea." She threw open a door and waved Nicola inside. "We've put you in here, and the bathroom is over there across the hall. Have a shower, if you like, but mind you go easy on the water. It's a scarce commodity in the outback." Then, as she walked away, she added over her shoulder, "That's not to say that *some* people don't waste water on a swimming pool, drought or no!"

Left alone, Nicola glanced around her small bedroom. It was simply furnished and spotlessly clean, with a white quilt spread on the bed and colorful mats on the cool tiled floor. She went to the window and stood gazing out. In the wired-off patch just outside there had been an attempt at gardening, but most of the plants were dead or wilted past redemption. Beyond, the paddocks took over, undulating country parched by the pitiless sun of the outback summer. Was it in this direction, she caught herself wondering, that Garth Rossiter's homestead lay? Despite the sticky heat, a shiver ran through her.

Slipping out of her navy suit, she lay down on the bed in just her bra and panties, thankful for the chance to relax completely for a few minutes. She felt deeply depressed. Nothing was as she had visualized it when she'd so blithely accepted the invitation to come to Australia for a holiday before taking a permanent job in England. The joyful reunion with Angie as she stepped off the plane at the airstrip hadn't materialized, and here at the Carson homestead there was none of the warm welcome she'd anticipated. Instead, the atmosphere here seemed to be seething with hatred and resentment against their neighbor, Garth Rossiter. Nicola bitterly regretted having unwittingly allowed herself to become involved with the man . . . not only for the Carsons' sake, but for her own sake, too. She knew that the memory of his passionate embrace, the thrilling promise of his lips, would take a long time to die . . . if it ever did.

Naturally, she hadn't reached the age of twenty-three without imagining herself to be in love now and then, and indulging in a certain amount of mutually pleasurable kissing. Deep in her heart, though, Nicola had always cherished the belief that when the time came and she fell *truly* in love she would experience an altogether different emotion. But how abysmally wrong she had been! Now she knew that such an emotion was no measure of love . . . for today she had been kissed by a man she despised utterly, and yet his kiss had been the most earthshaking revelation of her life. It had left her feeling shattered—and consumed with self-disgust that she could succumb so easily to a practiced womanizer. A shadow had fallen across her world with the discovery that she was so vulnerable. The instant Garth Rossiter had taken her into his arms she had been swept along in a daze of sensual excitement that had only been dispelled by the mockery in his voice as he released her.

Even now, despite a burning sense of shame, she felt erotically aware of her body and its need for fulfillment. If—heaven forbid—Garth Rossiter happened to cross her path again, he must be kept at a safe distance. Even the merest touch of his hand must be avoided for fear of the emotional chaos it would inevitably evoke in her.

With sudden resolution Nicola jumped up from her bed, threw open her suitcase to find her robe, and hurried across to the bathroom. She felt an urgent need to cleanse herself, to wash away all lingering traces of contact with him.

Standing under the shower, she ran a small quantity of water, carefully turned off the tap while she soaped herself, then ran a little more to rinse off the lather. Ten minutes later, dressed in a cool green cotton frock, she joined Mrs. King in the living room for the promised cup of tea.

Angie, returning an hour later, dusty from the paddocks in jeans and T-shirt, gaped in astonishment to find that Nicola had arrived. With an exclamation of delight she ran forward and gave her English friend a big welcoming hug.

"But how on earth did you manage to get here?" she demanded.

"Garth Rossiter," her aunt supplied, tight-lipped, before Nicola could answer for herself. "By a stroke of rotten bad luck, he was at Boolaroo airstrip."

"Oh, no!" Angie groaned. "Still, you're here now, Nikki, and that can't be bad."

Tony Carson walked in a moment later, accompanied by two bounding dogs, and Angie performed the introductions. To look at, brother and sister were considerably alike. Not tall, they were both rather stockily built and had the same sandy-colored hair. The fresh-faced look that made Angie appear so attractively bouncy and easygoing was perhaps, Nicola thought, just a little lacking in firmness for a man.

"I'm sorry about not being able to collect you," Tony told her apologetically. "The wretched utility truck wouldn't start. Again. Goodness knows what's wrong with it this time. And I guessed you wouldn't fancy riding a hundred miles in a Jeep on a road like that."

"I'm not a softie!" protested Nicola, with a laugh.

"No?" He ran an appreciative eye over her slim figure. "All the same, it would be a shame to risk bruising that kind of beaut upholstery."

"Trim your language," reprimanded his aunt. She added hastily, "I had a call from Jeff Anstey earlier on. He said he'd be over in the morning to fix the truck."

"Jeff Anstey?" queried Nicola in surprise. "Isn't that Mr. Rossiter's station manager?"

"That's right," said Angie. "I suppose Garth mentioned him to you?"

"Yes. You see, he . . . he happened to pass us on the road." Nicola felt herself flushing as she recalled the scene that Jeff Anstey must have witnessed as he came riding along on his motorbike.

"Jeff's a dead hand with anything mechanical," Angie explained. "A real wizard! We always get him to fix things for us."

"I see. And doesn't Mr. Rossiter object?"

Tony's face darkened. "If he does, he can go hang! In the outback we help each other."

Nicola felt it prudent not to mention the fact that Garth Rossiter had said exactly the same thing about helping each other—which had ostensibly been his reason for giving her a lift.

After another large pot of tea had been made and a plate of raisin scones consumed, Angie carried Nicola off to her room for "a good old yabber," as she called it, while she got changed. First, though, she dashed across to the bathroom to grab it before her brother did. When she returned she was vigorously toweling her hair. "Have to wash it every day, there's so much dust," she said ruefully, then went on with an apologetic grin. "I hope you didn't get too much grumping from Aunt Janet when you arrived. She can be a bit lemony these days."

Nicola shrugged it off. "I gather that your aunt isn't too well."

"No, she has these bouts of gallstone trouble which make her feel wretched. We've had to call the Flying Doctor service several times and they say she needs an operation, but she keeps putting it off." Zipping into her dress, Angie paused and gave Nicola a look. "Poor Aunt Janet, she's not had a very happy life."

"Losing her husband, you mean?"

Angie shook her head. "Well, no. She and Uncle Reg got on all right, but she married him on the rebound, and no one could pretend it was a love match. You see, she was jilted by Garth's father, Warren Rossiter. It seems that she and Warren were to be married that summer, but his parents were both killed in a fire that leveled their hotel when they were away from home at some sheep sales, and the wedding had to be postponed. But then instead of getting hitched to Aunt Janet, Warren Rossiter married someone else— the daughter of a rich banker from Sydney who was prepared to put money into the Kuranda station. It caused terrific gossip at the time, apparently. Aunt Janet went off to the city and in no time at all she married Uncle Reg, who had some sort of office job to do with opal mining. But then he died and she returned to live at Dandaraga."

"And she still feels bitter against anyone in the Rossiter family?" Nicola queried.

"Well, wouldn't you?" said Angie defensively. "Especially just lately, when she sees Warren Rossiter's son up to much the same calculating tactics as his father. We Carsons are nothing but a gnat in the eye to Garth. If he could buy us up and get a common boundary with the Drysdales' property, he could marry Zoe in the knowledge that eventually he'd be lord and master of the whole lot. Put together, the Drysdales' place and Kuranda—with our little bit of land in the middle—would make one of the biggest sheep stations in New South Wales. He's power-mad, is Garth!"

"But surely," Nicola ventured, "he doesn't have to own Dandaraga, does he? I mean, he could still marry Zoe Drysdale and run the two stations, even if you didn't agree to sell to him."

"But it would spoil the beauty of it for him. I'll show you a map sometime, and you'll see exactly how we divide up those two properties . . . like a thin slice of ham between two thick chunks of bread. No, Garth wants us out of the way, and he'll do just about anything to achieve it."

"And the Carsons are equally determined not to budge," said Nicola thoughtfully. "I can well understand that, Angie. Even if you have lots of problems here, the way things are, owning your own sheep station must be really terrific."

"I'm not so sure about that, Nikki. As far as I'm concerned, give me city life any time." Angie shot her an odd, questioning look. "But I guess that you're the sort of girl who would be really happy living here at Dandaraga, aren't you?"

It came to Nicola all of a sudden—and she wondered why it hadn't struck her before—that Angie regarded her as sister-in-law material. The thought filled Nicola with dismay. As far as one could judge on so short an acquaintance, Tony Carson was a very likable young man, and what's more he was a farmer—which in her eyes was the highest qualification for a potential husband. But Tony was not for her . . . never! That was something she knew with a feeling of utter conviction. But *why* was she so positive? Was it due to a certain weakness of character she sensed in Tony, a lack of determination, of decisiveness? Suddenly a picture flashed into her mind of Garth Rossiter's lean, chiseled features. There, she reflected, was as determined and decisive a man as you'd ever meet in a lifetime . . . but he was also offensively arrogant, overweeningly confident of his own superiority.

Thrusting the image away, she said with a nervous little laugh, "I'm only here for a holiday, remember. I'm certainly not planning to settle in Australia."

Angie shrugged. "No? What a shame! Still, you've scarcely arrived yet, have you? Time will tell!"

Aunt Janet served up an excellent tea of tender lamb cutlets with vegetables from the freezer and a peach gâteau to follow. In honor of Nicola's arrival Tony opened a bottle of Australian wine. As darkness fell and the curtains were drawn on the night they all grew

more convivial, the three young people laughing over a
game of cards, and then having a record session on the
rather scratchy stereo, while Janet King knitted steadily. They might easily, Nicola thought, have been
in the suburb of some big city, rather than miles
from anywhere in the vastness of the Australian
outback.

They retired to bed early, for the working day
at Dandaraga was a long one and they had to be
up at sunrise. It was only when Nicola was alone in
her small room that she became fully aware again
of their isolated situation. She discovered that the
night was full of tiny sounds . . . rustlings close at
at hand, the faint hum of the generator from an
outbuilding, and, far away, an eerie howling that
Angie had told her was the wild dog of the bush, the
dingo.

She felt desperately tired, yet she could not sleep.
After tossing restlessly for an hour or so, she slid
out of bed and went to the window. The night air
wafting through the flyscreen was pleasantly cool,
soothing to her bare arms as she stood there in her
cotton nightie. A huge orange moon hung in a sky of
velvety midnight blue, with no trace of cloud anywhere to mar its flawless perfection. And the stars
reached right down to the horizon, clear and bright—
the strange stars of the Southern Hemisphere, not
the familiar constellations she had always seen in
England.

Very faintly, she heard the sound of an engine . . .
a vehicle approaching? The sound grew nearer; then,
just when she thought the car must be coming to
Dandaraga, it began to fade again. Garth Rossiter,
going by on the high road? Returning home after an
evening spent with Zoe Drysdale, perhaps?

Nicola lingered at the window long after all sound of
the car had been swallowed up by the night. She felt
very small, very insignificant in the universal scheme of
things. Filled with a curious, wistful sense of yearning,

she found herself whispering inwardly, "If only, if only . . ."

Nicola slept fitfully, and she was already awake when the rest of the house stirred into life at first light. Angie had told her to lie abed as long as she liked, but she was impatient to look over the sheep station. She dressed hurriedly in jeans and a sweater, to the accompaniment of a cockerel that was crowing raucously just outside her window.

The three Carsons looked up in surprise as she entered the living room, where they were seated at breakfast.

"We didn't expect to see you this early," Angie told her.

"Who's objecting, though?" said Tony with a broad grin. "You're a very welcome sight." He leaned across to pull out a chair for Nicola. On the table there was a crock of brown-shelled boiled eggs, and Janet King pushed it in her direction, saying invitingly, "Help yourself, dear."

"Oh, no, thanks. I never have much for breakfast. Just a cup of tea, please, and perhaps a slice of—"

Mrs. King gave a loud snort of disgust. "At Dandaraga we eat hearty . . . we need to! So just you tuck in, my girl."

Nicola obediently took an egg and cracked it, dipping her spoon into the rich yellow yolk. It tasted delicious, as did the crusty home-baked bread, thickly spread with butter.

"What shall I do today?" she asked Angie.

"Well, I'll show you around the place a bit this morning, and afterwards you can either have a wander along the trail or settle with a book on the veranda, whichever you feel like."

"But I'd prefer to do some work," Nicola protested. "I want to make myself useful while I'm here."

"There's no need for that," Tony chipped in. "You're

supposed to be on holiday. Angie and I manage well enough between the two of us."

"You mean all on your own?" queried Nicola in astonishment. "Don't you have any staff to help you?"

He shook his head. "Nope . . . except for the two dogs. We cope, don't we, Angie? Besides, we couldn't afford any paid help. Except for the shearing, of course, but that's done by a traveling team of contractors."

Nevertheless, Nicola persuaded the brother and sister to let her give them a hand, saying that it would all be good experience for her. As the three of them were about to set out, Mrs. King—or Aunt Janet, as she insisted Nicola call her—noticed that she had no hat and tutted her disapproval.

"But I never wear a hat," Nicola protested. "I don't even own one."

"You've never felt the sun like it is here in the outback," she was told tartly. "It can be like a sledgehammer! Angie, find her something suitable."

Angie produced a white sailcloth hat with a floppy brim, and when Nicola put it on Tony gave her an approving grin and a whistle.

Nicola was disappointed to find that there were no horses kept at Dandaraga. Since first learning to ride when she was eight years old she had always managed, however spasmodically, to keep up her riding, and she'd been looking forward to the freedom of galloping across the open bush country on a spirited mount. But it seemed that these days motorized transport was more in favor in the outback, and Tony and Angie covered their territory in a bone-rattling Jeep, with the two kelpie sheepdogs, Cracker and Midge, piled in behind. They were friendly creatures, Nicola had found, and responded eagerly to a bit of petting from her.

Just before they started off Tony had slung in a roll of wire and a toolbag, explaining that there was some fencing in need of repair.

"We're responsible for that section of the boundary," he told Nicola as the Jeep bumped across a paddock of dusty red earth in which tufts of scrubby grass still managed to survive. "Mr. High-and-Mighty Rossiter will do it if I don't get it done soon, even though he can't wait for the day when the boundary will come down between his place and mine."

"Do you see much of Garth Rossiter?" asked Nicola, striving to keep her voice level.

Tony gave a bark of unamused laughter. "Too right we do! Not a week passes without that man finding something to beef about."

They dropped Tony at a place where the wire fencing was sagging badly, arranging to pick him up later on. Then Angie and Nicola, with the two dogs, set off on their way to a far paddock in order to drive the sheep grazing there to a fresh pasturage. But it could only be marginally better, thought Nicola grimly, and she wondered how it was possible for the animals to scratch enough sustenance from this parched, sun-baked territory. And Dandaraga, she remembered Garth telling her, was the best parcel of land hereabouts.

As Angie manhandled the Jeep over the bumpy ground, she said with a rueful laugh, "Poor Tony! He certainly goes on about Garth Rossiter, and with good cause, too. All the same, I sometimes wish that he'd give up and sell out to the wretched man."

"Oh, no!" Nicola gasped in horror. "I mean, being a farmer of any kind is something very special. Not just a means of earning a living, but a way of life. A marvelous way of life!"

Angie flickered her a reflective glance. "Guess I'm just not cut from the same cloth as you. It scares the pants off me, sometimes, when I realize how dependent Tony has become on having me around. Until recently it wasn't so bad, because Aunt Janet was more active and I could get away from the place sometimes. That's how I was able to come to England." She gave a deep sigh. "Honestly, Nikki, those three months I spent in England were the best I've ever known—and the best I'm ever likely to get."

"If you really dislike living here so much," Nicola said tentatively, "hadn't you better leave? I mean, you can't ruin your whole life . . ."

"But don't you see, by quitting I'd ruin *Tony*'s life," her friend pointed out unhappily. "He's been really great to me, Nikki, since Mum and Dad died when I was only a kid of twelve." She paused, then added with a note almost of pleading, "You do like him, don't you?"

Nicola wished that she had the courage to tell Angie straight out that nothing she could do or say was going to result in wedding bells for herself and Tony. But she was afraid of offending Angie by so blunt a statement, so instead she replied lightly, "Of course I like your brother. How could anyone help liking him?" Then she added weakly, "I shouldn't worry too much, Angie. Problems have a way of sorting themselves out. You'll see."

"I sure hope so! You know," Angie persisted, "I'd feel terrific if only Tony could find himself a wife to settle down with . . . someone who feels the same enthusiasm for the land as he does. He's worked so darned hard and he deserves a little happiness!"

Nicola felt a sense of panic take hold of her. This holiday in Australia, which she'd looked forward to as a great adventure, was turning sour on her. Would she have to spend her time here parrying Angie's attempts at matchmaking? And if that wasn't enough of a problem to cope with, it looked as if she'd have to expect Garth Rossiter to suddenly appear on the scene at any moment. They said he came often, if only to complain. Nicola dreaded the thought, certain that she would never be able to behave naturally in his presence. The very sight of him would send her senses reeling, and one penetrating glance from those vividly blue eyes of his would start tremors running through her entire body.

Yes, she dreaded the thought of Garth Rossiter coming—and yet she longed for it with a burning intensity. For with a single contemptuous kiss he had exposed an emptiness in her life that only he could fill. She hated him for that, because he had made her hate and despise herself. Until now, she had always believed that only a man whom she loved and admired would be capable of attracting her physically. But Garth Rossiter had proved that to be nothing more than foolish, romantic nonsense.

Resolutely, Nicola crushed down all thoughts of Garth and turned her attention to the job at hand. Handling sheep with well-trained dogs had always fascinated her, but never before had she actually taken part in the operation. She marveled at the way the two dogs, with only the minimum of shouted instruction, worked together in maneuvering the flock through a narrow gateway and then driving the sheep nearly a mile cross-country to another of the huge fields that were called paddocks here. Sometimes, in order to get from one side of the flock to the other by the shortest route, the dogs would actually leap up and race across the backs of the recently shorn animals. That didn't seem to cause the sheep the least concern, though when a dog confronted them on the ground they immediately fled in the intended direction.

At noon the two girls collected Tony and they all returned to the homestead for midday dinner. As they drove into the yard they heard the sound of an engine coming from one of the outbuildings. Through the open door Nicola saw Jeff Anstey straightening up from tinkering under the hood of an ancient Ford utility truck, a "ute," as it was called here.

"That's great, Jeff, you've got the ute going okay," Tony called. "What was the trouble?"

"It was the carburetor again," he replied. "I've managed to fix it for now, but it's sure to give you more problems before long. You'll have to get yourself some new transport, Tony."

"Yes, I suppose so," he agreed gloomily. "Anyway, thanks a lot, Jeff. Come in and have a beer when you've finished, right?"

While Tony went to put away his tool kit and Angie was fetching fresh water for the dogs, Jeff Anstey called to Nicola, "How're things going, Miss Wyatt?"

"Fine, thanks, Mr. Anstey."

"Call me Jeff," he said. "Everybody does."

"Very well, then . . . if you'll call me Nicola."

There was an easygoing friendliness about Garth Rossiter's station manager which she found herself responding to. He was rather older than she'd supposed from seeing him on his motorbike yesterday. Well into his fifties, she judged, and his wrinkled, deeply sunburned skin made him look even older.

"I've got a message for you from the boss," he went on cheerfully.

"Oh?" said Nicola warily.

"He said to tell you that any time you feel like a swim or a game of tennis, you're welcome to use the facilities at Kuranda. And likewise one of his horses—if you care for riding, that is."

Her heart thudding with excitement, Nicola told herself sternly that this was only a clever and devious move on Garth Rossiter's part in his battle with the Carsons. It was the old tactical routine of divide and conquer. If he could use his lethal charm to win her around to his viewpoint, it would be an extra weapon in his favor. Well, she wasn't such a simpleton as to fall for a trick like that!

"You can thank Mr. Rossiter for me," she said in a cool, lofty tone, "but I shan't be accepting his invitation."

"Why the dickens not?" asked Jeff, brushing away a persistent fly.

"Why not? I don't *have* to jump when Mr. Garth Rossiter chooses to pull the strings. I'm not a puppet."

41

Jeff Anstey grinned. "Too right you're not! Struck me when I passed you yesterday, though, that the boss was making headway."

Nicola flushed a raging scarlet. Quickly she turned her face away, praying that the wide brim of her hat would conceal her embarrassment.

"We had gone up on that ridge so that he could show me the lie of the land," she muttered unhappily.

"Oh, yes!" he said, his disbelief thick in his voice. Then, more seriously, Jeff continued, "Look, is it this to-do between Garth and the Carsons that's upsetting you? Ignore it, Nicola, like I do. I come over here whenever I choose, same as I always did. So does the boss, for that matter. The whole business is on their side, you know, and blown up out of all proportion."

"You'd have to say that, wouldn't you?" Nicola flared.

"I don't *have* to say anything," he protested mildly.

"But you're on *his* side."

"I'm loyal, if that's what you mean. Guess the boss is a man who inspires loyalty."

"Inspires, or *pays* for?" The bitter words were out before she could check them. She saw Jeff's face darken with anger, and she was full of contrition. "I'm sorry, Jeff, I didn't mean to be rude. I . . . I don't know what made me say that."

He was quick to grin and forgive her. "We'll have to put it down to the heat, eh? You're not used to it yet. Now let's go inside and get that nice cool beer that Tony promised." He gave her a straight look. "I should think about that invitation from the boss, though. There's not much for a girl to do around these parts except work, and you're supposed to be on holiday, I hear."

Ten minutes later, when Jeff roared off on his motorbike after quaffing a can of beer, Tony looked across at Nicola and asked suspiciously, "What were you two talking about for so long outside?"

Nicola was about to recount her conversation with

Jeff—or at least an edited version of it—but something held her back.

"Oh, nothing," she said with a casual shrug. "Jeff was just being friendly . . . asking about where I came from in England and so on."

The white lie, she told herself, was kinder and more diplomatic than the truth would have been.

Chapter Three

"We'll need to dress up on Saturday evening, Nikki," said Angie. "What will you wear?"

The two girls were sitting on the veranda after tea the next day, watching the sun go down in a blaze of splendor that gave the stark bush country a mantle of vibrant color. Tony had returned to work, using some of their precious water on the kitchen garden where he struggled to produce fresh vegetables for the table—without much success that Nicola could see. Aunt Janet was resting inside with her feet up, listening to a play on the radio.

"What's special about Saturday?" asked Nicola in surprise.

"Oh, I thought I'd told you . . . there's a party over at Kuranda station."

Nicola's surprise turned to sheer astonishment. "You mean that we're going to a party at Garth Rossiter's place?"

"Sure, why not?"

"Well . . . I thought you were hardly on speaking terms with the man, let alone socializing!"

Angie gave a rueful laugh. "You have to learn to see things differently in the outback, Nikki. There's no love lost between Garth and ourselves, but we get so darned few chances of getting together with other people that we can't afford to miss a party. It's not *Garth* we're interested in seeing; it just happens to be his turn to throw a party at his place. Folks will be coming from all around . . . distances of a hundred and fifty miles or more."

"I see." It was reassuring to know that there would be a whole crowd there. In fact, Nicola felt quite excited at the prospect of the party. She was interested in getting to know the people of the outback and how they lived, and this was an ideal way. There would be no need, she told herself, to have more than fleeting contact with her host for the evening.

"I've got a long dress in a sort of silky pink fabric," she told Angie. "Will that be suitable?"

"Stone sure it will! You'll knock the men for six with that perfect English complexion of yours." She gave a wistful sigh. "Wish I had your looks and figure. The best I can lay claim to is being the healthy outdoor type."

"And what's wrong with that?" asked Nicola.

"Just about everything"—Angie laughed ruefully—"when what you long to be is a sultry beauty . . . a sort of *femme fatale* like Zoe Drysdale."

"I suppose she'll be there?" queried Nicola, a sudden coldness invading her.

"Too right she'll be there! Not that she and Garth need the excuse of a party for getting together."

Nicola bit her lip and turned her face away. "What's she like?" she asked in a muffled voice.

"Zoe? Tall and slim and very, very sexy . . . a real bushfire blonde."

"What's that?"

Angie made a wry face. "A redhead, Nikki . . . a red-hot flaming redhead. She attracts men as if she were magnetized. Most of the availables hereabouts were buzzing round her like wasps round a jampot, and then she surprised us all by getting hitched to a Sydneysider."

"She's married?" asked Nicola in surprise.

"Was," Angie corrected. "Widowed now, and she's gone back to using her maiden name. The marriage only lasted about five months, and then he was killed in a car crash."

"Oh, that's terrible!"

Angie made a shrugging gesture with her hands. "He was roaring drunk, by all accounts . . . his usual condition. He was one of those penniless playboy types, and, my word, they had a merry time together spending her father's lovely money. We didn't see much of them around these parts, except for the odd flying visit home."

"Was Zoe in the car at the time of the crash?"

"Yep, and walked away with scarcely a scratch. That's her sort of luck."

"Luck!" protested Nicola. "When she'd just lost her husband!"

"Spare your sympathy. I doubt if Zoe shed many tears for him. Leastways, it didn't stop her playing around with the men again as if her marriage had never happened."

"Garth Rossiter . . . ?" said Nicola faintly, not quite knowing why.

Angie nodded. "There were plenty of others. Still are, is my guess. But Garth's the one she's playing for keeps."

On Saturday a light tea was served early in order to allow time to prepare for the party. Nicola was thankful now that, before coming to Australia, she'd splurged on the lovely pink dress, which really showed her slender figure to the best advantage. As she stood with it on before the wardrobe mirror, however, she wondered disconsolately how she would compare with the girl whom Angie had described as tall and slim and very, very sexy. But perhaps it was all the better, she consoled herself, if Zoe Drysdale outshone her to the point of making her completely insignificant. All the better if Garth Rossiter was given no cause to cast his eye over her in that slow, arrogantly appraising way he had. Let him give all his attention to the rich redhead he was all set to marry, and good luck to them! From the sound of it, they'd make a fine pair.

By the time they set off for Kuranda station the worst of the day's scorching heat had passed, and the blazing ball of the sun was sinking in the sky toward the distant western ranges. The three women were draped in linen dust rugs, to protect their dresses, and wore head-scarves. Judged by outback standards this was just a short drive, scarcely thirty miles. As they jolted over the potholes of the unmade track, Nicola was struck again by the stark, almost cruel majesty of the arid bush country. A pair of kangaroos watched them interestedly, not budging from the roadway, so that Tony had to veer around them. And a little farther on a bevy of long-legged, long-necked emus gave them an indignant stare before starting to run helter-skelter, their tail feathers bobbing comically.

Nicola had expected that Kuranda would be on a larger scale than Dandaraga, of course. But even so, she was astonished at the grandeur of Garth's sheep station. The house itself was set apart from all the other buildings, which Angie pointed out to her as the stables, shearing sheds, workers' bungalows, barns and storerooms, farm office, and even a shop. It was a long, low house, with white walls, which at the moment were turned to glowing orange by the setting sun.

"But it looks brand new," she commented in astonishment.

"Too right it is, too!" Tony grunted. "Four years ago Garth had the old ranch house torn down and started rebuilding from scratch . . . full air conditioning, the lot! Said he believed in having every modern comfort."

They drew up on a wide apron of gravel at the side of the house, where a dozen other vehicles of various kinds were already parked. A little way off Nicola glimpsed three light aircraft standing at the end of a runway of flattened bare earth. The sound of talk and laughter with a background of music could be heard coming through the long windows that opened onto the broad veranda that ran all around the house. Nicola could see a throng of guests inside, drinks in hand.

The main door was invitingly left open, and as they entered in a little group her eyes scanned the spacious hallway for Garth. She spotted him at once, chatting with a group of people off to the left. It wasn't just that he was taller than any of the other men present, but there was some indefinable quality about him that would let her pick him out in any crowd. Garth had noticed their arrival and he came over at once.

"Welcome to Kuranda!" It was a general greeting, yet there was mockery in his blue eyes as they met Nicola's gaze, and she knew that he was speaking directly to her—reminding her that she had scornfully denied the likelihood of ever having any reason to visit his homestead. In his maddeningly arrogant way he had said, "Oh, but you will, pommie girl." And now she was here, within only a few days of her arrival at Dandaraga. Unobtrusively, Garth allowed his glance to travel over her body in an insolent assessment, and she felt her cheeks burning at the memory of the intimacy that had passed between them.

"Tony, you'll see that Angie and Aunt Janet get drinks, won't you?" he was saying affably. "I'll just take Nicola round and make a few introductions."

She felt a swift stab of panic. But to object would make her look foolish, she decided despairingly, so she meekly allowed herself to be led away. Garth's hand gripped her elbow as he steered her forward, and it felt as if a potent electric current were flowing through to her. When he pressed a glass into her hand her nervousness made her swallow half the contents in a single gulp. It was gin and tonic, she found, and very strong. Not her usual drink at all.

"Jim and Irene, meet Nicola Wyatt, fresh out from England. Brian, this is Nicola . . . Frank, Tess, Rosemary . . . Nicola is staying with the Carsons . . ."

In a daze she smiled at people and murmured a few words of greeting. Everyone was so friendly, so welcoming. Garth guided her over to the veranda, where a pleasant-looking middle-aged woman was sitting with two or three of the older guests. At once she broke off her conversation and said with a smile, "Don't tell me—you'll be Angie Carson's young friend. Nicola, isn't it? Jeff told me about meeting you."

"Mary is Jeff's wife," Garth explained. "Just as Jeff runs the sheep station without much help from me, Mary rules the roost here in the house."

There was a general laugh, and Mary Anstey said lightly, "Don't believe a word of it, my dear. Nobody—but nobody—tells Garth Rossiter what to do!"

Except a certain redhead, thought Nicola bitterly.

Before moving on, she received a pressing invitation from Mary Anstey to visit her any time she was over at Kuranda.

"Our bungalow is just past the stables," Mary informed her. "It's the first one you get to, so you can't miss it. Just drop in for a cup of tea, or whatever, any time you feel like it."

There were still more introductions. Invitations were showered on Nicola to visit, to picnic, to attend a barbecue supper. And there were Christmas parties, too, already being planned . . . it really did seem so odd, Christmas in the middle of summer!

Altogether, Nicola met so many new people that their faces became a blur in her mind. And then, striking through the blur, a pair of green eyes gleamed.

"Zoe Drysdale," she heard Garth introducing. "She and her father are the Carsons' neighbors on the other side, as I expect you already know."

Zoe was everything that Angie had said, and much more. She was dressed in a gleaming silk gown that plunged deeply between her breasts, its emerald-green color a perfect complement to the molten-red hair that swung about her shoulders in luxuriant waves. A bushfire blonde, Angie had described her.

The green eyes surveyed Nicola, assessed her, dismissed her.

"So you're staying with the Carsons," Zoe drawled. "Perhaps you can knock some sense into their silly heads."

Anger gave Nicola her voice. "What's that supposed to mean?" she demanded.

Her green eyes flashed derisively, but Zoe didn't bother to answer the question, as if underlining the fact that she considered this girl from England too unimportant to merit further attention. Laying possessive fingers on Garth's arm, she said languidly, "Darling, do come and settle the date for us to dine with the Smithsons. I know it's a bore, but Carol is getting so tiresomely pressing."

Garth nodded and glanced at Nicola. "Will you excuse me?"

"Of course," she said coolly. "You mustn't let me keep you."

He hesitated a moment longer. "Just move around and mix with people," he instructed her. "It's that sort of party . . . very free and easy."

"Come on, Garth," cut in Zoe impatiently. Her hand, with those long red fingernails, looked like a claw on his arm, Nicola thought bitterly.

Left alone, she glanced around for Angie or Tony, or even Aunt Janet, but none of the Carsons was anywhere to be seen. Then she felt a hand on her shoulder and turned to find a young man beside her . . . a big, broad, hefty type, with the healthy outdoor look of these outback people. And already, Nicola noted ruefully, he was carrying several drinks too many.

"Ho, ho!" he exclaimed with a chuckle. "So our little cousin from the old country is all on her lonesome. That won't do! Were you looking for me, sweetheart? I'm Brian, remember?"

"Actually," Nicola told him distantly, "I was wondering where Angie had got to."

He grinned at her foolishly. "Reckon I could tell you where she is, darling, if I wanted to."

"Then please do."

"Make it worth my while?" he asked, with a heavy wink.

"Oh, don't be silly," she responded, managing to smile at his nonsense. "Come on, tell me."

Brian paused a moment, then said, "She's down by the pool. Some of them were thinking of having a swim."

Nicola was surprised, not realizing that Angie had brought any swimming gear. "Where is the pool?" she asked Brian.

"I'll take you there," he offered.

"No, really, there's no need. If you could just point me in the right direction . . ."

"Better let me show you," he said, taking a firm grip on Nicola's arm. "It's getting dark outside now and you might lose your way. That would never do, would it?"

Leading her out onto the veranda, Brian took her down a short flight of steps and along a path through a shrubbery where fragrant white and yellow flowers shone in the fast-fading light. It was a clear night, and the immensity of the sky was studded with jewel-bright stars. As they moved farther from the house the sounds of the party diminished to a low murmur, and there was only silence. Feeling suddenly uneasy, Nicola came to an abrupt halt.

"Where is the pool?" she demanded suspiciously.

Brian gave a soft giggle. "Who cares about the pool, darling? There are better things that you and I can do, eh?"

Nicola sighed with exasperation. "I suppose you thought it very funny bringing me out here like this on a pretext . . ."

"Not funny," he corrected. "Best idea I've had in a month. Minute I clapped eyes on you I thought, My word, she's a real beaut . . . the sort of sheila a man could have a good time with. Come on, darling, let's make lovely music together." Before Nicola could take evasive action, he caught hold of her hand and pulled her against him.

"Stop that," she protested, shaking herself free and stepping back.

"What's the matter?" he demanded thickly. "Hey, are you Tony Carson's Mabel by any chance?"

"What do you mean . . . his 'Mabel'?"

"Y'know, his girlfriend."

"No, of course I'm not!" she retorted. "I'm a friend of his sister's, that's all."

"Well, then . . ."

"Well nothing!" she said furiously and started back to the house. To her dismay Brian grabbed her and swung her around again. With a smothered giggle he clasped her to him and started kissing her. Nicola struggled frantically but to no avail. He was far too strong.

A voice cracked like a whiplash out of the darkness. "Okay, Brian, that's enough! Let go of her at once!"

"What the . . . ?" he spluttered, as he released his grasp on Nicola. "Oh, it's you, Garth. Hey, did you have to come out and break it up just when I was making progress?"

"Get back to the house," Garth commanded in a firm, level voice. "And I'd advise you, Brian, to grab something to eat at the buffet. You've had too much to drink on an empty stomach."

"Hey, are you suggesting that I'm—" he began to protest, but Garth cut across him, curtly this time. "On your way, sport!"

"Thanks, Garth," said Nicola shakily, after Brian had stumbled away into the darkness. Then she added, untruthfully, "But there was really no need for you to intervene. I could have handled the situation."

"You think so?" he queried mockingly. "You would have got a lot more than you bargained for."

"Oh, don't exaggerate," she protested furiously.

Garth took an impatient breath. "When a fellow like Brian has been working hard all week with his father's sheep and no female company . . . well, come Saturday night he's in a mood to break out and go wild. A girl with an eminently desirable body like yours is a big temptation to a man, and you can't altogether blame him for being in an almighty hurry."

"He got me out here by a trick!" Nicola exploded indignantly.

"Spare me the excuses!" snapped Garth. "You came with him willingly enough. I watched you leaving, and Brian certainly didn't have to drag you."

"But I . . . I'd explained to him that I was looking for Angie, and Brian told me that she was out by the swimming pool."

"What the deuce would Angie be at the pool for, at this time of night?" he asked scornfully. "She was inside dancing when I left the house just now. What did you want Angie for, anyhow?"

"Oh . . . nothing, really. I mean, I was left on my own, and—"

"And Brian conveniently happened along! Only you didn't realize that you were dicing with danger. Here in the outback, pommie girl, life doesn't follow the same cozy little rules as it does in the cities, and any female who flaunts her physical assets is liable to get exactly what she deserves. Especially a girl like you who can so easily be set on fire with just a single kiss."

"You're being utterly ridiculous as well as insulting!" she flared, seething with anger. "I'm going back inside."

"Just a minute!" Garth reached out and grabbed her arm, and the remembered grip of steel made her gasp aloud. Against the star-pricked sky his tall figure was a dark, menacing silhouette, but there was enough light to let her see the glitter of his eyes.

"Sorry if I came along a bit too soon and deprived you of your fun," he drawled. "Still, I can always put that little matter right."

Suddenly her heart was thudding wildly like a jungle drumbeat. Trying to sound calm and controlled, she said lightly, "I don't know what you're talking about."

"Then I'll show you."

With a swiftness that robbed Nicola of breath he pulled her to him, his hand pressed into the small of her back as he clamped her body against his in an intimate embrace. Then his mouth came down on hers in a kiss of brutal, sensual possession, his lips forcing hers to part before their relentless pressure. Gradually his hold slackened; he was no longer claiming her body by right of force but from mutually mounting desire. Nicola felt herself melt against him, molding her feminine softness against his muscular strength, and she was excitingly conscious of the stir of arousal in him. Slowly, as if of their own volition, her hands came up and clasped around his shoulders, kneading the firm flesh beneath his jacket, drawing him closer, ever closer. . . .

Somewhere on the outer fringe of her consciousness she was aware of music throbbing on the still night air. But nothing else mattered except herself and Garth kissing here in the fragrant garden. It was as if the two of them were the very center and pivot of the entire universe.

Then, as Garth finally released her from the circle of his arms, he said with a low laugh, "My word, you are an eager sheila! You wanted that even more than I had guessed."

Nicola felt herself go ice cold, and the next instant burning hot as a flush of shame raced through her body.

"You . . . you're utterly despicable!" she stammered.

"Despicable? For kissing a pretty girl? That's a strange charge to make against a man."

"You know perfectly well what I mean." Her voice was a husky murmur, but charged with deep feeling. "You . . . you degrade what should be beautiful between a man and a woman into something cheap and sordid. It's all some huge joke to you, isn't it? I suppose, with your distorted mind, you get a feeling of power to . . . to . . ."

"To what?" he inquired mockingly.

She caught her breath. "Anyway, it won't work again, you can be sure of that. I'm armored against you now . . . I've got your measure."

"Dangerous words, pommie girl! It doesn't pay to challenge a man in that sort of way."

She ought to have turned on her heel and walked off with what dignity she could muster, she knew that. Yet something held her there, something forced her to stay and argue with him—a refusal to admit defeat.

"You won't take me by surprise again," she said defiantly. "That's what you rely on, isn't it? Catching a girl off guard?"

"Not at all," he returned equably. "If you like, I'll give you fair warning that I'm going to kiss you so you can be fully prepared. The result will be precisely the same. How about after a count of ten?"

"No!" she cried in alarm, and took a quick step backward. She felt a low, prickly bush snag at her long skirt, but she was past caring.

"So you admit that I'm right?" he said triumphantly. "You admit that you'd succumb the instant I took you into my arms, however determined you might be to hold out?"

"You're wrong!" she insisted, against the wild pounding of her heart.

Garth's hand shot out and his cruel grip was on her shoulder. "So I have to give you another practical demonstration? Is that what you're angling for?"

"Leave me alone!" she said, a sob cracking her voice. "Let me go this minute, or I'll—"

"I'm not letting you go until you've admitted that I'm right," he returned implacably. "Admitted that, whatever your puritan little mind might be telling you, your sexy body is screaming out with desire for me."

"That's not true! I despise you utterly."

"Whether or not you despise me doesn't come into

55

the matter," he declared. "You want me; that's what it's all about."

"I don't—I don't!"

Garth said impatiently, "You leave me no alternative but to stage a repeat performance."

He meant it, Nicola knew. And now it was too late to beat a dignified retreat, even if her trembling legs would have allowed it. She stood transfixed, knowing that at all costs she must hold him at bay. At all costs she must fight her own weakness, her own treacherous yearning to be swept again into his arms and experience that deliriously sweet enchantment of the senses.

By an immense effort she managed to inject a bite of scorn into her voice. "Very well, if it feeds your arrogant male vanity, I admit that you could probably overcome my resistance and—"

"Only *probably?*" he queried, his tone carrying menace.

"It's . . . quite likely," she amended. Then, because even that admission clearly wasn't going to be enough for him, she added wretchedly, "Very well, then. Yes, you could!"

"Honesty at last," he observed, not attempting to keep a gloating triumph from his voice.

"I hope you're satisfied now," she said bitterly. "I suppose it never bothers you, Garth Rossiter, that the people over whom you ride roughshod end up by feeling an intense loathing for you and everything you stand for."

"Over whom am I supposed to have ridden rough-shod?" he inquired, and again she saw the faint glitter of his eyes. "I get the impression that we're no longer just talking about women."

"You must have enemies all over the place," Nicola threw out wildly. "Men like you—ruthless empire builders—invariably do."

"The people who oppose me are usually their own worst enemies," he remarked flatly.

He could still amaze her by his incredible arrogance.

"Have you the least idea," she asked witheringly, "how disgustingly conceited that sounds?"

"Conceited or not, it happens to be true."

"Are you suggesting that Tony Carson is his own worst enemy for trying to defend his heritage against the sheer power of your money?"

"Tony hasn't done very well with his heritage, as you choose to call it. Very probably," Garth added laconically, "because the poor chap's heart isn't in sheep farming."

Nicola gasped in astonishment. "That's the complete opposite of the truth. Tony is absolutely dedicated to making a success of Dandaraga. If he wasn't, why should he refuse to sell out to you?"

"Obstinacy?" Garth suggested lazily.

"Guts!" she contradicted. "Sheer guts! I really admire Tony for standing up to you and your bullying tactics."

"How nice for Tony," he commented in a derisive tone, "having such a delectable champion to come rushing to his defense. But nothing you say will alter the fact that Dandaraga is badly run-down these days and that it needs a hefty injection of capital to get it on its feet again. It's good land—that's what the name means in aboriginal language, 'good country.' But it's too small a station to make economic sense under modern conditions. Much better to incorporate the place under a larger umbrella."

Nicola gave an ironic laugh. "We all know why you want to get your hands on Dandaraga, Mr. High-and-Mighty Rossiter. It stands in the way, doesn't it? It interferes with your grand plans for the future."

"You appear to know a great deal about me, Nicola."

"Indeed I do!" she said, "You'd be surprised!"

"You've not succeeded in surprising me yet, pommie girl. The surprising thing would be if you hadn't learned

57

all there is to know about me—plus a lot more that's been invented—within hours of arriving in the district. We run a very efficient bush telegraph here in the outback—something you'd do well to remember," he added significantly.

"Why should it bother *me?*"

"Because," he explained with an unpleasant chuckle, "you've been out here in the dark garden for quite a long time now, first with Brian, then with me. Most of the women inside will have taken note of that fact, and they'll have drawn their conclusions about you."

Mercifully, the night concealed Nicola's flaming face. "I only came out to look for Angie," she protested.

"You'd have a job to convince anyone of that, considering that Angie hasn't set foot outside the house since she arrived here."

In her wretchedness Nicola sought to hit back at him. "No doubt Zoe Drysdale will be one of the women to have drawn conclusions about me being out here with you," she pointed out.

"Are you concerned about that possibility?" he inquired interestedly.

"Of course not. Why should I be concerned?"

"Why indeed?" he mocked.

Nicola longed to pierce the armor of his self-conceit. She said thickly, "I wish you joy of Zoe. I expect you've met your match in her. She looks as if she has a temper to raise the roof."

"Look who's talking," he chided. "It's been my experience of women that quickness of temper is usually an indication of an intensely passionate nature. That's certainly borne out in your case."

Nicola had an urge to strike him across the face, but he would only claim that it proved his point. Somehow controlling her seething anger, she turned and started back to the house. But once again he restrained her, the grip of his fingers bruising the soft flesh of her bare arm. His voice was different, no longer mocking but stern and in deadly earnest, it seemed.

"For your own sake, Nicola, you'd better remember that I've done you a big favor tonight."

"How on earth do you make that out?" she asked impatiently.

"Brian wasn't playing for peanuts," he explained. "If I hadn't noticed you come outside with him and followed, you'd have had yourself a lot of trouble. He wouldn't have been content with just kissing you, that's for sure."

"Don't be ridiculous. Do you imagine that I'd have let him . . . ?"

"You couldn't have stopped him—any more than you could have stopped me if I'd had a mind to carry on. Face it, with a body like yours that catches fire in a man's arms, it needs a lot of self-control for him to stop short of the limit." Garth released her then, and Nicola's hand instinctively flew to cover the spot where his fingers had dug in so cruelly.

"Okay," he clipped, "the lecture's over now. You can scuttle off back to safety—but don't forget what I've said."

Still Nicola stood there, tense and unmoving, all strength apparently drained from her legs. She hated this man as she had never hated anyone in her life before. And yet he unleashed in her the most bewildering emotions. He was standing so close that she could feel his breath stirring her dark curls, feel the heat pulsing from his masculine flesh. She had an almost irresistible urge to reach out and touch him, to lay her hands on his broad shoulders and rest her cheek against the hard-muscled wall of his chest. Seeking what? A feeling of safety, of tranquility? But there could be no tranquility for her with Garth Rossiter, only the torment of awakened desire. And that spelled danger! He had put a curse upon her, arousing her to an acute awareness of needs and cravings she had only dimly known before. Against her will she longed desperately to feel his lips on hers again, longed to tangle her fingers in the sun-bleached hair that curled so crisply at his neck, to mold herself intimately against the hard contours of his superbly virile body.

When she felt him touch her again she almost cried out with the sudden tautening of tension. But it was only to turn her around in the direction of the house.

"Go on, get out of here!" he said, flipping her lightly on the backside. There was an odd thickness in his voice as he added in an undertone, "Go, for pity's sake, before I lose all grip on myself."

Nicola slipped in through a side door and reached the bathroom unnoticed by any of the other guests. It took only a moment to check her hair and smooth down her dress. But for minutes more she sat before the mirror until her heartbeat was steady enough for her to feel able to return to the party.

Tony pounced on her the moment she went in through the lounge door. "Nicola, I've been looking for you everywhere," he said. "I'm afraid we'll have to be leaving soon, because Aunt Janet's not too clever."

For a second she didn't grasp his meaning. More of that Australian slang again, she thought. Then: "You mean she's feeling ill? Oh, dear, that's rotten luck. Is there anything I can do to help?"

"I don't really know. She's lying down at the moment, and Angie's with her."

He led Nicola along to one of the guest rooms at the end of a passageway. Angie opened the door to his knock. She looked very anxious.

"Aunt Janet's real bad," she said, frowning. "It's one of the worst bouts she's ever had. I think we should call the Flying Doctor and see what he suggests."

Tony nodded. "Right! I'll find Jeff Anstey and get him to put a call through on the transceiver. I'll be as quick as I can."

"It's the usual trouble, I suppose?" whispered Nicola, following Angie into the room where Aunt Janet lay on the bed, covered with a blue counterpane.

She was moaning softly and her face was very pale, beads of perspiration visible on her forehead.

"Too right we know what it is," said Angie with a sigh. "Those wretched gallstones! All this past year the doc's been telling her that she should go into hospital and have them out. There's nothing to it these days, he assured her, but things could get dangerous if she waits."

"Why won't she agree to have it done, then?" asked Nicola. "Is she scared?"

"Not Aunt Janet—she's not scared of anything." Angie shrugged. "No, it's sheer stubbornness. She says it's because she can't leave Tony and me to manage on our own. I keep telling her that's a lot of nonsense, but Aunt Janet won't listen to reason."

Tony was back within minutes, an unusually determined expression on his face.

"Doc says there's to be no messing around this time, she's to go into hospital right now," he informed them. "If not, it could perforate. They're sending a plane out from Broken Hill as soon as one is available. It should be here in a couple of hours."

When this news was passed on to the patient she nodded in acceptance, too weak to argue. "Guess I should've listened before," she said in a feeble whisper.

There was a tap on the door, and Garth entered. "Jeff has just told me," he said with a frown of concern. "I'm sorry. And I gather there's some delay with the plane."

Tony nodded. "It's a busy night, seemingly."

"Well, no problem. I'll fly Aunt Janet in myself; it'll be a lot quicker. Matter of fact," he added crisply, "I've already informed the Flying Doctor service that they needn't come."

Aunt Janet had heard that, and she began to stammer a protest. Garth cut across her, gently but firmly. "No buts. You need medical attention just as soon as possible. Angie, you tell her."

"It does make sense, Aunt Janet," Angie confirmed, though Nicola noticed that she looked unhappy at the idea of having to accept any favor from Garth.

"But I don't want to be beholden," the older woman grumbled.

"We don't use that word in the bush," Garth said brusquely. "You ought to know that, being a native outbacker yourself. I'll go and get the plane fueled and readied up. You be ready in . . . say, ten minutes."

"Do you think I might go with her?" asked Angie thoughtfully, glancing at her brother. "It seems awful to send her off on her own."

Tony glanced questioningly at Garth, who was at the door. He nodded briskly. "That's okay by me. There's room for two passengers. See you outside, then."

It was all arranged with bewildering speed. Tony and Angie between them carried their blanket-wrapped aunt to the front entrance while Nicola followed behind with her handbag. Outside, Jeff Anstey was waiting with a station wagon and drove them all the two or three hundred yards to where the plane stood ready. There were hurried goodbyes, the door slammed, and the plane's engine burst into throaty life. Then, with a roar, it was skimming down the runway and lifting into the night sky. It turned in a half circle and headed away, its navigation lights fading into the darkness. As Nicola and Tony walked back to the homestead, Jeff switched off the runway lights.

"What do we do now?" she asked.

Tony sighed, sounding uncertain. "Garth said we were to return to the party and tell the others to continue with the fun and stay just as long as they like. Guess I'm not really in the mood for staying, though. How about you and me getting back to Dandaraga? Angie will be giving us a radio call later on, when she has some news."

In all the worry and bustle about Aunt Janet, Nicola hadn't paused to give thought to what the emergency arrangements would mean for herself. Returning to Dandaraga, she would be entirely alone in the homestead with Tony, the nearest neighbor miles away. She shrugged the problem off as soon as it occurred to her. Good heavens, in the circumstances she'd be badly needed at the little sheep station, at least until Angie was able to get back. Indeed, it was fortunate that the crisis with their aunt had arisen while she was around to help.

"Yes, Tony, let's head back straightaway," she agreed.

Tony was obviously relieved. "I'll just go and explain what's happening, and then we'll be on our way."

For the first few miles of the journey they discussed Aunt Janet and her illness, but when that subject was exhausted they fell silent. The utility truck's headlights cut a swath into the darkness, and now and then they disturbed a kangaroo. Once a pair of phosphorescent eyes gleamed eerily.

"A dingo," said Tony absently. A moment later, he cleared his throat and remarked, "When I was looking for you earlier on, Nicola, someone said that you were outside in the garden with Garth."

"I was searching for Angie," she replied in automatic defense.

Glancing covertly at Tony's profile, she saw in the faint green light from the instrument panel that he was frowning.

"Why did you imagine that Angie had gone outside?" he asked.

"Because someone told me she had," Nicola said quickly—and too fiercely. She continued with a casual shrug, "But then Garth found me and explained that I'd got it all wrong, so I came in again."

"You were a mighty long time about it," Tony grunted, after a lengthy pause.

Nicola offered no comment. The vehicle lurched

over a bad pothole in the unmade road as he went on. "What was Garth saying to you?"

"Oh, nothing much." It sounded patently untrue, and she could hardly expect Tony to believe her. She tried again. "As a matter of fact, we had a row. I went for him, rather, and he attempted to justify himself."

"Oh, how?"

Nicola bit her lip. "He said . . . well, he tried to make out that the incorporation of Dandaraga station into his place would make economic sense."

"Which is true," Tony remarked with an underlying note of bitterness.

"Maybe. But, as I told him, there's a lot more to life than economics." Nicola felt that, in the circumstances, it was perfectly excusable to stretch the truth a little. These were sentiments she might very easily have expressed, given the opportunity. "I said that farming is a whole way of life to some people, not just a way of making lots of money. But Garth didn't seem to see that point of view."

"No," said Tony thoughtfully, "I don't suppose he did." The wheels skidded on a patch of thick dust, then gripped again. "And that was all?"

"What do you mean, 'all'?"

"Garth didn't . . . well, try anything?"

"Why should he?" she parried, wishing to heaven she could deflect Tony from this embarrassing subject.

"Well, he has quite a reputation where women are concerned." Tony sounded faintly admiring and envious, she thought. "Zoe is only the latest of a long string."

Nicola gave an edgy laugh. "If they all had Zoe's fantastic looks, Garth would hardly rate me worth a second glance."

"I don't know," Tony argued. "I think you're a very attractive girl, Nicola."

She laughed again, and it sounded forced. "Thanks for the compliment."

"But I mean it," he asserted.

Nicola didn't reply, and she was thankful that Tony let the subject drop there. At last they reached Dandaraga, and Cracker and Midge ran out to greet them with loud welcoming barks. Nicola patted and fussed over them for a moment, giving Tony time to open up and put the lights on. When she went in, she said briskly, "I think I'd like to get straight to bed."

"I'll bring you in some tea, if you like," he offered.

Nicola shook her head. "I don't want any, thanks."

He nodded. "Well, goodnight then. I'm staying up by the transceiver till Angie calls."

"Oh, yes, of course," she said, then added guiltily, "Er . . . wake me up, won't you, if there's anything special to report."

Nicola was in bed within a few minutes. Though she felt exhausted, she knew that she wouldn't be able to sleep. With her mind churning over the evening's events, she lay and listened to the great stillness of the bush. Gradually she drifted into a doze.

She jerked back to consciousness at a soft tap on her door. Tony called, "Are you awake, Nicola?"

"Yes, Tony. Have you any news?"

Instead of just putting his head around the door he came right in and perched himself on the edge of her bed.

"Angie's just been through," he said, "and I thought you'd like to know that everything's okay. They're preparing Aunt Janet for surgery first thing in the morning. No problems, apparently; it's all quite straightforward."

"Oh, that's a relief!"

"Yes, isn't it?"

Tony lingered, and in the light spilling in from the hall he seemed to be studying her face. After a while he reached out and with his finger stroked a tress of hair back from her forehead. He seemed uncertain, hesitant, and Nicola wondered how she could bring this

65

awkward situation to an end. She gave a big, exaggerated yawn, and luckily Tony took the hint.

"Well, then, I'll see you in the morning," he said huskily. "Sleep tight, Nicola."

With a swift movement he bent and kissed her gently in the center of her brow. Then he was gone, shutting the door quietly behind him.

Chapter Four

"I hope you didn't mind me telling Angie to stay over," said Tony, giving Nicola an anxious glance. "Only it seemed sort of unkind to leave Aunt Janet all on her own when she's bound to be feeling pretty groggy."

They had just received news over the radiotelephone that Aunt Janet's operation had been satisfactorily completed and that the patient was doing well. Nicola hadn't given much thought to when exactly Angie would be back, having been busily on the go since she got up this morning at sunrise. First there had been breakfast to cook, a meal of outsize proportions: ham and eggs and chops, with plenty of hot tea. It must be the outdoor life, she supposed, but already in the short time she'd been at Dandaraga she'd learned to enjoy a hearty breakfast herself. Afterward she had hastily done a round of housework before going out to join Tony in one of the paddocks where he was watering sheep. What with one job and another, the morning had slipped by until it was time for them to return to the homestead to receive the promised call from Angie.

"No, of course I don't mind, Tony," she assured him. "Angie must stay on as long as she feels she ought to. We can manage between us."

"It doesn't really seem fair to you," he muttered apologetically. "You're supposed to be here for a holiday, and now you're coping with both Angie's and

Aunt Janet's jobs. But you mustn't . . . well, overdo it, Nikki. I mean, I can handle most things on my own."

"Don't worry, Tony," she said with a bright smile. "I'm enjoying myself. Honestly."

He gave her a long, thoughtful look, his hazel eyes so admiring that Nicola felt quite embarrassed.

"You know, I really believe that you *are* enjoying yourself here," he remarked. "Strange, isn't it, that Angie, who was born and bred in the outback, doesn't find the life all that exciting, whereas you, a city girl born and bred and not even Australian, should take to it like a duck to water."

Feeling acutely uncomfortable with the way this conversation was heading, because she thought she could see into Tony's mind, Nicola said dismissively, "I expect it's just the novelty. It'll wear off after a few weeks and I'll be longing to return home."

Tony's face clouded for a moment; then he said with a little chuckle, "We'll just have to make sure that doesn't happen, won't we?"

Nicola shooed him outside at that point, saying that she herself would remain and prepare the midday dinner, another substantial meal. She soon had a joint of lamb sizzling in the oven and moved to preparing vegetables. The potatoes were cooking when she heard a vehicle draw up outside. Tony, back again so soon? It looked, she thought ruefully, as if she might have a certain amount of trouble with Angie's brother during these few days they were to be alone together.

But it wasn't Tony. She was startled to hear Garth's deeply resonant voice calling, "Anybody home?"

She quickly tugged off the apron she was wearing and ran her fingers through her dark curls as she hurried out to the hall just as Garth stepped in through the front door. He was dressed casually, as she had first seen him, in a checked shirt and khaki drill trousers that fitted tightly over his slim hips. The sight of him brought Nicola a jumble of emotions that she couldn't begin to untangle.

68

"Hallo," she greeted him, trying to keep her voice on an even keel. "Have you heard the news? Mrs. King's operation was completely satisfactory and she's doing fine."

"Yes, I checked for myself," he said coldly. His blue eyes narrowed to chips of ice and he demanded harshly, "What the devil is going on here?"

"What . . . what do you mean?" Nicola could feel herself wilting before his unexplained anger.

"I'd have thought it was perfectly obvious what I mean," he rasped. "I could hardly believe my ears when I arrived home last night and learned that you'd gone back to Dandaraga with Tony."

"Where else did you expect me to go?" she stammered, still bewildered.

"Anywhere but here, for heaven's sake! And then, on top of that, I'm told this morning that Angie is proposing to remain at Broken Hill for a while. So is it any wonder that I ask what the devil's going on?"

Garth's attack had unnerved her, but somehow she gathered herself together and hit back at him. "As far as I can see," she said disdainfully, "it's not the slightest business of yours."

With an obvious effort, he spoke in a more reasonable tone. "I'm only telling you for your own good, Nicola. What on earth do you expect people to think, knowing that you and Tony are holed up here alone together?"

"If that's the sort of nasty minds people around here have," she retorted furiously, "then I don't care what they think.'

"Well, I do!" he snapped.

"That's just too bad, isn't it?" Nicola said sarcastically. "But I'm afraid it cuts no ice with me. You may be the autocratic lord and master over everything that goes on at Kuranda station, but what you happen to approve of or disapprove of counts for nothing here—not yet. And never will—Tony will make sure of that!"

Garth shrugged her outburst aside. "If you have any

sense at all, you'll see that what I say is right. I'll tell you what, I'll ask Mary Anstey to come over and stay here for a few days. She won't mind, and—"

"You'll do nothing of the kind," Nicola protested, outraged. "If you did that it would convey to everyone either that I'm a completely incapable nitwit or that Tony and I are afraid of gossip. Which we're not!"

"Brave words!" he sneered. "But you might not be so cocky when your reputation is in shreds."

"Oh, for pity's sake," she burst out, "you seem to forget that we're in the *nine*teen eighties, not the *eight*een eighties!"

"That's no excuse for being permissive," he snarled.

"Who says that I'm being permissive?"

"Are you denying it? Maybe—just maybe—nothing has happened so far. But are you seriously expecting me to believe that nothing *will* happen?"

About to deny the suggestion hotly, Nicola checked herself. Why should she give Garth that satisfaction?

"I'm not asking you to believe anything," she said. "You can think whatever you like for all I care."

Garth caught her by the shoulders and shook her roughly. "You little fool, can't you see that you're playing with fire?"

She twisted in an effort to escape his harsh grip, but to no avail. "Let me go—you're hurting."

He took not the slightest notice, and the look of cold anger in his eyes made Nicola feet quite scared.

"You may imagine it's amusing to fool around with Tony's emotions," he grated, "but you'd better think again. For a long time now he's been stuck away here, trying to make this place pay its way, with no one for company but his sister and his aunt. And now, suddenly, he finds himself all alone with an outstandingly attractive girl. Are you blind?" he finished, suddenly releasing her. "You're sitting on a keg of dynamite, Nicola."

"You seem to imagine that all men are like you and think of nothing but sex," she said bitterly.

"Men," he said darkly, "are men!"

Nicola felt so furious that she was beyond weighing her words. "Whatever you think Tony and I might get up to, why should it bother you?" she cried and added recklessly, "Are you jealous or something?"

Garth's head jerked around and his eyes blazed blue fire. "Jealous!" he echoed in a savage voice. "What on earth do you mean by that?"

Nicola quailed before the rage she had unleashed, but she wasn't going to back down now. "I meant, are you jealous because Tony's in a position that you'd like to be in? Does it eat into you that another man might succeed in getting what you so badly want for yourself?"

Garth threw back his head and gave a bark of laughter. "My dear girl, if I wanted you that badly, I'd take you, make no mistake about that. And there's nothing you could do to stop me. Or would want to do, I might add."

"Honestly, you're arrogant! If you think for one moment that I'd allow you to—"

"Your head might try to say one thing," he ground out savagely, "but your body would be screaming another. Don't forget that I've held you in my arms and felt you tremble, felt all your resistance melt away."

"Not again!" she cried vehemently. "Never again!"

"Is that a challenge?" He took a step toward her and, flinching back, Nicola found that she was pressed against the wall.

"Of course it isn't," she protested. But he had noted her nervousness and his eyes glinted in triumph.

"So you're afraid," he mocked. "Afraid of yourself."

Nicola felt the sheer animal magnetism of the man threatening to overcome her senses. She tried to summon up willpower enough to give him a telling, dismissive answer, to walk away from him in cold disdain. But she was powerless to move. All she could do was to shake her head weakly.

"Let us see you make use of this iron will you claim

to possess," he said with heavy sarcasm. "How will you react when I touch you, I wonder—as a solid block of ice or as a screaming virago?"

From utter stillness, watching her with intent eyes, he suddenly moved and took her possessively into his arms. Nicola fought back at him wildly, but only for a few brief seconds. Then it was herself she was fighting, doing battle against her own treacherous instinct to yield, even to respond. In moments all her resistance had crumbled to nothing and she was utterly pliant, accepting with humiliating joy the bruising pressure of his lips on hers, the vise-grip of his hard-muscled arms, the harsh savagery of his male body crushing hers.

Feeling as though she were sinking into a whirlpool, she clung to him desperately, arching her body to meet his, all thought of protest swept away before the sensuous delight of his kiss. No longer needing to hold her captive, Garth's hands began to roam her body, caressing the soft curves of her flesh and finally coming up to cup the roundness of her breasts, finding the sharp-pointed nipples through the flimsy cotton of her shirt.

"No!" she cried in sudden protest as a terrifying surge of longing shafted through her.

Surprisingly, Garth let go of her at once, stepping back and raking long fingers through his thick mass of sun-bright hair.

"No, it wouldn't suit your book to let Tony catch you with me, would it?" he asked in a tone of humorless sarcasm.

"What . . . what are you talking about?" she stammered.

"As if you didn't know! He's just driven up."

"Just driven up," she echoed dazedly. "I didn't realize that."

"Oh, no? You were having a ball kissing me until you suddenly heard the Jeep come back, and don't try to deny it."

She prayed that Tony wouldn't come into the house for a few moments, that she would have time to pull herself together. Breathing raggedly, she turned to a mirror on the wall and tried to tidy her dark curls. Her face was strangely pale, she noted, her eyes huge and luminous.

Tony didn't linger outside. He could scarcely have paused to do more than check the dogs' water trough before entering the house. As she heard his footsteps on the veranda steps she cast a beseeching glance at Garth.

"Don't say anything, please!"

"Maybe he ought to know," was the curt reply.

"For pity's sake," she begged.

Tony didn't look at all pleased at finding them together. "I saw your vehicle outside," he said to Garth ungraciously.

Nicola held her breath as she awaited Garth's response, hating him, yet silently imploring him. He said easily, "When I heard that Angie was staying in Broken Hill I came over to see if I could offer any help. I was suggesting to Nicola that Mary Anstey could come and keep house for you."

Surprised, Tony glanced at Nicola, who gave a tiny shake of her head. Tony appeared to be relieved.

"Decent of you, Garth," he muttered. "But we won't need to trouble Mary. Anyway, how would you manage without her? Or Jeff, either?"

"Jeff and I wouldn't be trying to cope all on our own as you are," Garth pointed out. "You forget that at Kuranda station there are plenty of other people to share the load."

"Yes, I suppose so," Tony temporized. "All the same, Nicola says that she doesn't mind . . ."

"Of course I don't mind," she confirmed quickly. "We can manage perfectly well between us."

The look Garth turned on her was like a body blow. "Well, then," he said in a scathing voice, "I'll leave you

73

to get on with it." His eyes were burning into hers, yet Nicola couldn't look away. "You know where I am, if you want me . . . for anything!"

As the door closed after Garth's retreating back, she fled to the kitchen. She had planned to serve glazed carrots to go with the meat and potatoes, but they were still uncooked. She slid them away out of sight and went into the storeroom to fetch some frozen peas instead. The burst of activity helped her to control her trembling limbs, for which she was grateful.

Tony came through and stood in the doorway, watching her. "How Garth likes to try and rule the roost around here," he grumbled. " 'I'll lend you my housekeeper,' he says, just as if Mary is some piece of property to be moved around as he sees fit. She herself isn't expected to have any say in the matter."

"I don't think Garth meant it quite like that," Nicola found herself saying. "He knows Mary well enough to be able to speak for her; that's all he meant, I'm sure."

Tony grunted and said sulkily, "Standing up for him now, are you?"

"No, not really. It's just . . ."

"Don't trust him an inch," he warned her. "Garth can be smooth-tongued enough when he wants—especially with an attractive girl. He just likes to prove his power over women; it's a challenge to him. So keep that well in mind, Nikki."

"I'm not interested in Garth Rossiter," she said, her voice muffled.

"Well, you stay that way," Tony advised. "If he's determined to play around, let him do it with Zoe Drysdale. She's the sort to give him what he wants and come through unscathed."

"Oh, for heaven's sake," Nicola snapped, banging the saucepan she was holding down on the stove. "See to the peas, will you? I'm just going to . . . to do my hair."

In her room, she sat on the edge of the bed while she tried to get a grip on herself. Tony's remark had sent her spinning into a vortex of jealousy such as she had never believed possible. And yet . . . why *should* she be jealous? She loathed and despised Garth Rossiter, and Zoe was welcome to him! It was humiliating to be so much in the grip of such purely physical urges where Garth was concerned. By using the expertise of a born philanderer he could sweep away her feeble resistance and transport her into dark, unknown realms of sensual desire where modesty and self-respect had no place, where the very idea of pure love and an enduring relationship between a man and a woman was laughable. With clenched fists she promised herself that never again would she succumb to those urges. Bleakly, she acknowledged that she would have to ensure that she was never again placed in a position where she and Garth were alone together; otherwise she would never be able to trust herself to reject him.

When she emerged from her room Tony had dished up the vegetables and was carving the leg of lamb. He gave her a wary, questioning glance, but his remark concerned the weather prospects.

"It seems hotter than ever today. Sometimes this heralds the end of a drought. I sure hope so!"

For the following three days she and Tony were cooped up entirely alone together, without visitors of any kind. Their only contact with the outside world was a daily chat over the transceiver with Angie, who reported on Aunt Janet's continuing good progress. Nicola detected a curious kind of excitement about Angie, which she attributed to her being able to spend some time leading an urban life in Broken Hill, the "Silver City" of New South Wales.

On the third such evening, Angie tentatively made the suggestion that she should postpone her return to Dandaraga even longer.

"You see," she said, "Aunt Janet is to be discharged from hospital in a few days' time, but she'll never agree to stay on here by herself, and if she comes home we'll have a job to stop her from doing too much. So I thought that if I took a double chalet here at this hotel, I could make sure that she rests up properly."

"Right!" Tony agreed readily. "You keep her there, Angie, until she's really fit and well."

As he said this he glanced at Nicola for confirmation, and she nodded her head reluctantly. In truth she felt dismayed that Angie's absence was to be extended further, but how could she say so? Alone here with Tony at Dandaraga she felt she had to watch every single word she uttered in case he misconstrued it as an invitation to get on romantic terms with her.

"Of course you must stay on, Angie," she insisted uneasily. "You're not to think of coming home until your aunt is fully recovered."

Angie made a sound that was like a smothered giggle. "Say, it's dead lucky, isn't it, that you two get on so well together? I mean, if you hadn't taken to each other the situation could be a bit tough, right?"

"We get on just great," Tony confirmed. "Don't we, Nikki?"

She laughed nervously and avoided a direct answer. "I'm certainly learning a lot about sheep that I never knew before, Angie."

"That's great. But don't go overdoing it, Nikki. Remember that there's more to life than tending sheep. Tony, just you make sure that she takes time off to relax. Why don't you drive her into Boolaroo with you next time you go, and have a meal at the hotel—a meal she doesn't have to cook herself? Give the poor girl a break!" There was another smothered giggle. "You never know, it might pay dividends."

Tony acted on his sister's advice next morning. "I've got to go into town today to pick up some supplies," he informed Nicola. "Why don't you come along, too, as Angie suggested?"

"Surely we'd better not both go off and leave the place?" she protested. The thought of a few hours on her own without Tony, without having to be constantly on her guard, seemed something of a respite.

"Why not?" he replied cheerfully. "Dandaraga won't come to any harm. The sheep are okay, and I'll feed the dogs before we leave. They'll be happy enough roaming around for a few hours with no work to do for once."

Nicola sought for another excuse but then thought, Why not? Though she genuinely loved the empty expanses of the bush country, there was no doubt that she was growing altogether too introspective. She badly needed an injection of other people; it would be a tonic just to exchange a few words with complete strangers.

"Right, then, I'll come!" she told Tony.

"That's great," he said. His lighthearted mood suddenly disappeared and his expression was serious, rather soulful. "You and me, Nikki, don't you think . . . ?"

She cut across him, saying briskly, "I'll just clear the breakfast things while you go and see to whatever needs doing outside. I'll be ready whenever you are."

When they reached Boolaroo after a hot and tiring journey, it seemed odd to Nicola that what had struck her on disembarking from the plane as a tiny, isolated township now seemed a bustling hive of activity by outback standards. In the main street there must have been at least twenty people going about their business or stopping for a neighborly chat. Tony parked outside the hotel and they entered the blessed coolness of the lounge. Never had Nicola so much enjoyed an iced tea with lemon. It was lovely, too, to join in a friendly conversation with the bartender and the handful of other customers.

Refreshed, she found the blazing sun outside more bearable when they went to collect the supplies Tony had come for: a new battery to replace the one in the Jeep, which was on its last legs, he told her gloomily, and various spare parts for the ancient diesel generator at Dandaraga, which Jeff Anstey had promised to overhaul for him. Tony pulled a long face when presented with the bill, and she noted how reluctantly he signed the check. They took the opportunity to stock up with groceries, Nicola having made a hasty list of what was needed before leaving, then headed back to the hotel for a meal.

It was a small, simply furnished dining room, but cool and pleasant, and the aroma wafting from the kitchen was appetizing. But as they walked in Nicola suddenly halted in dismay. Seated at a table near the window were Garth Rossiter and Zoe Drysdale.

Tony muttered something in an undertone. Like her, he seemed to want to retreat. But they'd already been noticed, and Garth rose to his feet to greet them. Today he was wearing a crisp white shirt, which contrasted vividly with the mahogany brown of his skin. No man had any right to look as devastatingly handsome as that, Nicola thought wretchedly, as her heart began to beat a tattoo against her rib cage.

"Well, well, this is quite a surprise," he drawled. "What are you two doing in town?"

In a sullen voice Tony explained that they'd been picking up supplies, and Garth went on affably, "Won't you join us for lunch? Zoe and I haven't ordered yet."

Nicola protested instinctively, "Oh, but we—"

"Come on!" he pressed, and pulled two chairs from an adjoining table, setting them in place. Zoe watched all this with smoldering dislike in her green eyes, but she decided to adopt an outwardly friendly attitude.

"Yes, do join us!" She glanced at Garth with an intimate smile and added roughishly, "After all, Nicola, you and Tony can't pretend you don't get enough of one another's company. It must be quite a romantic idyll at Dandaraga at the moment, with just the two of you."

Garth's face was expressionless as he cut across her.

"Zoe is off to Sydney on the afternoon flight and staying overnight."

Tony, who wasn't looking at all embarrassed by Zoe's arch comments, Nicola noted ruefully, gave a sigh that was something between envy and admiration. "What it is to be rich! You think nothing of flying off to Sydney whenever you feel like it, do you, Zoe?"

"Life here in the outback would be quite insupportable if I couldn't get to civilization now and then," she said, with a delicate lift of her shoulders. They were magnificent shoulders, the smooth skin tanned to a lovely honey-gold, revealed by the low-cut white linen dress she was wearing. Her gorgeous red hair was swirled up into a chignon against the heat, showing the slender column of her neck. "I've been telling Garth," she went on, "that it's high time he took another break . . . it's all of two months since we had that week in Melbourne together, darling. I don't *have* to return tomorrow, if you'd like to change your mind and come with me after all."

Garth shook his head. "I've far too much on hand. But there's no sense in you rushing back if you don't have to, Zoe. Why not stay over a few days while you're about it?"

Nicola saw the brief flash of anger in Zoe's green eyes, but the other woman gave Garth a fond smile. "How could I enjoy myself, darling, thinking of you sweating it out back here in this dreadful heat? And it's all so unnecessary, too. Heaven knows what you pay that man Anstey for if he can't take over from you more often and leave you free to get away when you feel like it."

"Jeff has *his* work to do on the station, and I've got mine," he replied with an easy laugh. How patient Garth was with Zoe, Nicola reflected bitterly, showing none of the irritation he displayed with her.

"But you *own* the place," Zoe protested, pouting.

"All the more reason for putting all my energies into it," he returned equably. "Isn't that right, Tony?"

It was a snide remark, a taunt, and Nicola wasn't surprised that Tony flushed red. She felt furiously angry with Garth for rubbing salt into the wounds. Poor Tony was up to his neck in debt to the bank, and putting his lifeblood into running Dandaraga . . . all the while facing the galling knowledge that it might be for nothing in the long run. And biding his time, waiting to pounce when things became really desperate, was Garth Rossiter. Like some predator of the jungle, she thought with a shiver. He'd buy Dandaraga for a fraction of what it was really worth, marry Zoe Drysdale, and end up as one of the biggest sheep barons in the whole of New South Wales.

In an attempt to conceal her stormy feelings, Nicola had been making a show of carefully studying the menu. When she looked up again she found that Garth's gaze was upon her, the clear blue eyes gleaming with mockery. Fervently she wished for a hole in the floor that would swallow her up.

The waitress came to take their order then, and as she departed Zoe remarked in an audible voice that she was looking forward to having some decent food in Sydney.

"I think I shall go to the Provençal for dinner this evening," she mused. "You remember, Garth darling. That charming little French restaurant we discovered last time."

Tony, his cheeks still a little flushed from Garth's gibe, asked wonderingly, "Are you really going all the way to Sydney just for one night, Zoe?"

"Of course! Where else can I get my hair decently styled?" she demanded. "I wouldn't dream of putting myself in the hands of the sheep shearers around here."

It was a thoroughly uncomfortable meal from beginning to end. Nicola had little appetite, yet she hardly dared glance up from her plate for fear of finding herself staring into Garth's hard, disapproving eyes. Zoe talked more than anyone else, and almost everything she said seemed to underline the fact that she and

Garth were on intimate terms. Time and again she reached out to touch his bronzed hand where it rested on the table while she talked animatedly of past incidents the two of them had shared . . . as lovers, she was proclaiming loud and clear.

Eventually, to Nicola's intense relief, the time came for Zoe to catch her plane and she and Garth departed. When Tony called for his bill, he was informed that it had already been settled by Mr. Rossiter.

"Rotten showoff!" he grumbled to Nicola as he pushed his billfold back into the pocket of his jeans. "Does he imagine that I can't even afford to buy you a meal?"

"Don't let it bother you," Nicola advised soothingly. But it was advice she herself found hard to take. Garth Rossiter always managed to find a way of intruding on her life and spoiling things.

There were one or two other bits and pieces of shopping to do, and then they returned to the utility truck for the homeward journey. But Tony had scarcely driven more than a hundred yards when the vehicle started jerking erratically and making a loud screeching noise.

"Oh, blast!" said Tony with a groan, as he quickly braked and switched off the engine. "What's up with the wretched thing now?"

"Sounds suspiciously like the clutch to me," remarked a laconic voice from a few feet away, and they both swung around in their seats to see Garth strolling toward them. When he went on to inquire, "Have you been having trouble with it lately?" Tony looked uncomfortable.

"Well, it has been slipping a bit," he admitted. "I realized that it would need relining soon."

"Then it seems you left the job too long. It doesn't pay to be so casual in the outback, where a breakdown could leave you stranded in the middle of nowhere. You were just lucky it happened right here in town."

"Spare me the lecture!" Tony protested, flushing.

"I've got enough on my plate without that." He sighed and looked around, as if hoping for inspiration.

Garth said crisply, "Well, get out, man! Nicola can take the wheel while you and I push the ute to the repair shop."

Why should they meekly obey orders from him? she thought furiously, but she had to acknowledge that what he said made good sense. Indeed, there was little else they could do. Five minutes later the truck was rolling onto the forecourt of the town's one and only garage. The proprietor emerged from the big corrugated-iron shed, wiping his hands on an oily rag. When the problem had been explained he started the motor and drove a few yards, then examined the engine and finally pronounced his verdict. The whole clutch assembly needed to be replaced.

Even worse was to come. It seemed that he didn't have the necessary spare parts in stock, not for such an out-of-date model. They had to wait while he did some checking around on the phone, and eventually he located what he wanted at another workshop in a township almost two hundred miles away across the bush.

"How soon can you get them here, Sam?" asked Tony, looking thoroughly wretched.

The man pushed back his cap and scratched his head thoughtfully. "A couple of days should see them here. But it would speed things up some if you could drive over and collect them yourself, Tony. I could lend you a wagon, and you'd be back again before morning. Then I'd get to work on it first thing, and I guess you'd be on your way home by this time tomorrow."

Tony was looking positively haggard now, and Nicola could well imagine what was going through his mind. While he still floundered in an agony of indecision, Garth had it all worked out.

"Tony, you take Sam's wagon and collect the parts," he said briskly. "Meantime, I'll take Nicola back to Kuranda in the plane with me, and she can stay the night with the Ansteys. Don't worry about Dandaraga; I'll send a man over to check on things and see that your livestock is okay and feed the dogs."

Both Nicola and Tony at once started to protest against this idea, but Garth retorted with a clipped "Have either of you got a better suggestion to make?"

That silenced them. Nicola realized that, come what may, they would be forced to accept Garth's assistance in one form or another. But she wanted at all costs to avoid being under a personal obligation to him—or being alone in his company.

"There's not the least need for me to come back with you," she argued. "I'm sure that, in the circumstances, Tony will be very grateful to you if you can send a man over to Dandaraga when you get home, but I . . ."

"Yes? What exactly do you propose to do with yourself? inquired Garth sarcastically.

"I . . . I could go with Tony."

But even Tony himself objected to that idea. "I'm not taking you a couple of hundred miles and back on that terrible road; I know what it's like," he said.

"Then I'll stay here . . . at the hotel."

Garth was impatient. "What would be the point?" he snapped. "Don't be stubborn, Nicola. You know perfectly well that what I'm proposing is the only sensible thing to do."

She glanced at Tony for support, but he shrugged apologetically. "Garth's right, Nikki. You don't know a soul here, so it wouldn't be much fun for you. And Mary Anstey really would be happy to have you; she doesn't get all that much female company."

"So it's finally agreed?" Garth asked tersely. "Thank heaven for that! Come on, Nicola; let's get moving. You can pick her up at Kuranda, Tony, on the way home tomorrow."

"Yes, okay."

To Nicola, it was far from being okay. She felt deeply resentful of the way the two men had settled things between them, as if she had no say in the matter. She feared, though, that no further protest on her part was likely to make any difference. Even if she could change Tony's mind, Garth had a way of overriding any plans that weren't precisely along his lines.

"I'll see you tomorrow, then, Tony," she murmured. To which he responded with a faint, abstracted smile.

Garth's plane was waiting for him at the airstrip, fueled and ready to go. He thrust Nicola aboard and climbed in himself. He checked over the controls, made sure that she'd clipped her seat belt on correctly, and immediately asked for clearance for takeoff. In a matter of moments they were airborne.

Garth didn't attempt to talk, for which Nicola was thankful. She watched the bush country sliding past beneath them and couldn't help but marvel. Having actually set foot on the arid, sun-baked soil, she could now appreciate far more clearly what she was seeing from the air than she had on her flight from Sydney. She could *feel* the savage grandeur of it all now, this primitive outback territory that stretched forever into the blue-hazed distance, mile after endless mile.

Garth said suddenly, "The bush must have come as a surprise to you after your lush green English countryside."

"Well, yes," she admitted. "I wasn't expecting it to be quite as dry as this."

"Once we get rain—if we get rain—the whole landscape will be transformed in a day or two."

"Is the drought likely to break soon?" she asked.

"Who knows? It's impossible to tell in this crazy climate."

By plane it took an amazingly short time to cover what had taken more than two hours of fast driving by road. When they were nearly there, Garth said, pointing downward, "From up here you get a good idea of the lie of the land. Dandaraga is straight ahead . . . see it? To the right lies Kuranda, and over to the left is the boundary of the Drysdales' place."

It all lay spread beneath them like some giant sketch

map, and Nicola realized as never before how effectively the Carsons' little station separated the giants on either side—a long and narrow sliver of land keeping them apart. Had he deliberately flown on this course to let her see for herself how hopeless it was for Tony to try and fight off the inevitable amalgamation?

"Way over there," said Garth, "is the Drysdale homestead. Can you see it?"

She followed the direction indicated by his finger. Far off, where the sun-scorched land and the brazen sky seemed to merge into a strange and insubstantial mist of unreality, a mirage floated, a large white house of many gables, with the greenness of trees around it like a cradle.

"It . . . it looks very grand," she murmured.

"Very grand indeed," he responded. "It was built some hundred and fifty years ago with the vast fortune made by the first selector, who was granted the land by the government. The house is a real Gothic extravaganza!"

"You sound as if you don't much approve," Nicola observed, and found herself not altogether displeased by the thought.

"It's not for me to approve or otherwise," he said. "The place isn't mine."

"Yet!" she said viciously, and nearly bit off the tip of her tongue in regret.

Garth turned in his seat to look at her, and his blue eyes were alight with derision. "Your claws are showing, Nicola."

She could not outstare him, so she turned away to look out the window again. The scene below them tilted suddenly as Garth banked into a turn; then in a few minutes they landed on his own private airstrip at Kuranda. He taxied to the end of the dirt runway and cut the engine.

As they were walking to the house Jeff Anstey appeared from the office building and gave a cheery wave.

"I'll just go and have a word with him," Garth said, excusing himself.

Nicola felt awkward at being thrust like this on Jeff and his wife. But she consoled herself with the memory of Mary's pressing invitation to visit them any time, so presumably they wouldn't mind too much.

Garth was back in a couple of minutes. "Sorry, Nicola," he said lightly. "I'm afraid it quite slipped my mind that Mary is away visiting her daughter today."

She stared at him in dismay. "But . . . what do I do now?"

"Oh, there's nothing to worry about," he said. "It's just that she won't be back until late. You see, the Ansteys' daughter, Fiona, who's married to the under-manager of a cattle station at Murrawbri Dam, has recently had a baby. Mary's been going over for the day once a week lately, but it's only a four-hour drive and she'll be back by midnight."

"Midnight!" gasped Nicola in horror, wondering how she was going to fill the long hours that stretched ahead of her.

Garth took hold of her arm and gave her a reassuring smile. "You're getting upset about nothing," he said in an untypically friendly voice. "Come on, we'll go to the house and I'll show you where you can freshen up. Then we'll get ourselves some tea. After that . . . I'm sure that we'll find things to do to occupy the evening agreeably. You'll see, Nicola; the time will simply fly past."

Chapter Five

"How about a swim?" Garth suggested as he and Nicola sat over tea on his shady veranda.

Unwisely, she made the first excuse that came into her head. "I can't . . . I haven't any swim gear with me."

"Hardly a serious obstacle," he drawled. "The men are all still at work, so there'll be nobody around the pool to spy on you."

"If you mean," Nicola began hotly, "that I should swim in the nude, I—"

"Why not?" he cut in. "I'm certain that you've got nothing to be ashamed of. In fact, very much the reverse." He let his eyes travel slowly and assessingly over her slender figure, then added with a lazy smile, "Weren't you taught that one should always give pleasure to others when it's within one's power?"

"You're being ridiculous!" she snapped. "And offensive."

"I'm sorry," Garth responded, unabashed. "I thought I was paying you a compliment."

"You're enjoying this, aren't you?" she asked him bitterly.

"I'd be the last person to deny it. Why shouldn't I enjoy the prospect of spending a few hours in the company of an extremely attractive girl?"

"I meant that you're enjoying making fun of me." Nicola clenched her hands tightly beneath the wickerwork table. "I suppose you had this all worked out. I don't for a minute believe your story about forgetting that Mary Anstey wouldn't be here today."

The blue eyes danced with devilry. "It's lucky I did forget, isn't it? Otherwise you might not have agreed to come."

"I most certainly wouldn't!" she affirmed.

"With the consequent result," he reminded her with a sardonic smile, "that at this moment you'd have been stuck in a hot and uncomfortable hotel, with no one to talk to and a boring evening ahead of you. As it is, you'll have comfort and pleasant company, good food—and various agreeable pastimes."

"If you don't mind," she said, knowing it sounded rather feeble, "I'd as soon just sit here on my own and . . . and read."

He gave her a look of pained surprise. "Is that how you pommies repay an act of kindness?" he inquired interestedly. "I don't wish to rub in your obligations to me, I was only too glad to assist you and Tony in a difficult situation, but I do think that in return I can fairly claim the pleasure of your company, Nicola. We don't see so many people here in the outback that we can afford to miss an opportunity."

"I'm quite sure," she returned swiftly, "that you never go short of company."

"I seem to remember," he said thoughtfully, "that you made that remark to me once before, when I drove you from the airstrip on the day of your arrival, and I readily conceded the point. Especially as it related to *female* company. But as I pointed out to you at the time, it's always nice to have an extra option."

Darn the man, thought Nicola furiously, he always had an answer to everything she said. But there must be some way of shaking his overwhelming self-confidence. She seized on the first thought that entered her head. "I very much doubt," she said, "if Zoe would take kindly to hearing you say that."

Lazily, Garth flicked his wrist to glance at his watch, and Nicola noted the glint of the fine blond hairs that grew on his sun-bronzed forearm. "Zoe will have landed in Sydney some time ago," he observed. "That's a long way from here."

"But she'll be back tomorrow."

"Tomorrow," he pointed out calmly, "is another day, Nicola. Now, about that swim?"

"I told you, I can't."

He grinned at her with an air of unanswerable triumph. "If you insist on being prudish, pommie girl, I'm sure Jeff will fix you up with something to satisfy your maidenly modesty."

"How can Jeff . . . ?"

"His daughter always leaves a few of her things with her parents for when she visits," Garth explained. "Among them there's certain to be a swimsuit." He surveyed Nicola's shape through narrowed eyes. "Fiona's vital statistics are much the same as yours, I'd say—without somehow adding up to quite the same enticingly proportioned whole."

Before she could make any further protest he was off down the veranda steps. There was nothing Nicola could do but wait for his return. The whole atmosphere was so different from Dandaraga, she noted resentfully. The gardens surrounding the house were well maintained and watered, full of brightly colored shrubs and massed roses. A passion flower twined luxuriantly up a pillar supporting the veranda, and when she reached out to touch one of the exotic purple blooms it felt velvety to her fingertips. Overhead in one of the wattle trees a kookaburra, or laughing jackass, as those curious birds were called, started a steady chuckle of laugher that set Nicola's nerves on edge.

A couple of minutes later Garth reappeared with Jeff, who was carrying a wisp of something yellow in his hand.

"Here you are, Nicola," Jeff said pleasantly. "Not

the height of the current season's fashion, perhaps. Fiona has had it three years or more. Still, I'm sure it will do."

It turned out to be a diminutive bikini, and she took it from Jeff in dismay. She had been intending to stand firm and oppose any idea of swimming, but it seemed churlish to reject Jeff's offering when he had gone to the trouble of hunting up the swimsuit for her. Anyway, she had to admit that the thought of diving into cool, clear water was infinitely appealing after days of enduring the relentless heat. She had a feeling, too, that to go on refusing would, in a perverse sort of way, give Garth even greater satisfaction, because it would betray the fact that she was afraid to be in such an informal situation with him. Somehow she had to overcome that fear and force herself to give the impression of being totally indifferent to his nearness.

So she made herself say brightly, "Thanks a lot, Jeff. By the way, I'm sorry to be landing myself on you and Mary tonight."

"Don't spare it another thought," he told her with a friendly smile. "Mary will be only too delighted. As I am!"

Garth removed the plastic cover of the pool, which was there to stop evaporation, and the sight of the rippling rectangle of azure water was enticing. In the chalet that he indicated Nicola changed into the borrowed bikini. Fiona, she decided ruefully, must be a little on the skinny side, for the flimsy yellow fabric was considerably stretched on herself, the garment consequently becoming even more minuscule than its designer could have intended.

She emerged nervously from the chalet with the intention of diving quickly into the pool and submerging her nearly naked body beneath the water, but she was diverted by a burst of applause from Garth. He was standing just across the pool from her, and she thought with an involuntary catch of breath that, stripped for swimming, he looked even taller and more magnificently male than ever. He wore tight-fitting white swim trunks, and his upper body and his strong muscular legs were just as deeply bronzed as his face and arms. There was a fuzz of golden hair on his broad chest, and she caught the glint of what looked like a St. Christopher medallion.

Garth gave her a slow, unhurried assessment, letting his eyes linger on every curve and swell of her body. Then, in that maddeningly assured drawl of his, he said, "It may interest you to know, Nicola, that even my most optimistic expectations have been excelled."

Nicola felt herself blushing all over. She wished she had the confidence to dive in nonchalantly and gracefully with Garth looking on, but in her present state of nerves she was afraid she would muff it and end up pancaking on the surface of the water in total indignity.

"I doubt," he went on slowly, measuring his words, "if you could have succeeded in choosing a more flattering swimsuit if you had actually bought it for yourself."

"I certainly wouldn't have bought this one," she said ungraciously.

"No? Something even more revealing, perhaps?"

Through gritted teeth she muttered, "As a matter of fact, my own swimsuits are all one-piece."

"Really? That seems rather an uncharitable attitude—depriving the males who happen to be around of an innocent form of pleasure. But then," he went on, as if debating a serious topic, "you women know all there is to know about exciting the interest of the opposite sex. I've got to admit that a certain element of mystery can set fire to the imagination. Whatever might be said in favor of your present outfit—and there's a great deal!—an element of mystery isn't one of them. For all that bikini conceals, you might just as well dispense with it completely."

Nicola's body, so pale in contrast to his, was flaming

now with embarrassment. In desperation she turned and dived into the pool—and just as she had feared, she made a complete hash of it. The impact left her winded, and she gulped and spluttered.

Garth dived, cleaving the water neatly, and was beside her in a moment. "Are you okay, Nicola?"

"Of course I am," she lied, then turned her back on him.

They both swam around for a while, Nicola taking great care to keep a safe distance between them. Presently Garth heaved himself out of the pool and sat on the side, letting his feet dangle, the droplets of water glinting on his bronzed skin like diamonds in the sunlight. Nicola remained where she was, sticking to the breaststroke, which was the one she did best. As she swam up and down the pool she was aware of Garth's eyes following her, watching every movement she made. She willed him to get back into the water so that she could seize the chance to jump out and head back to the chalet. She couldn't bear to climb out now in full view of those sardonic eyes of his.

At long last he dived in again and Nicola hastily scrambled out, making an undignified dash for shelter. When she was dressed once more—wishing she had something less ordinary than the jeans and shirt she had worn to town—she was astonished to find Garth already changed and waiting for her.

"Well, then, what do we do now?" he inquired amiably.

"I'd really prefer to be left on my own," she stated.

"We've been through that before," he said reproachfully. "You owe me, Nicola—you owe me at least these few hours of your company."

"And you're a man who exacts his pound of flesh, aren't you?" she flashed.

"Is there anything wrong in expecting reciprocation for a favor done?"

She sighed and said crushingly, "I might have known

that you're not a person to do something for nothing. There's a Japanese proverb I heard once that applies very aptly to you: 'When you buy a vase cheap, look for the flaw; when a man offers favors, look for the motive.'"

Garth considered that, nodding in appreciation. "Neat! It reminds me, though, of the Latin tag: 'He'—or to fit the case in point, *she*—'receives more favors who knows how to return them.'"

"I shan't accept any more favors from you," Nicola informed him with a lift of her chin.

"Don't speak too hastily," he advised. "The time may come when you'll regret saying that."

"I very much doubt it!"

In their verbal tussle, she had scarcely been aware of the direction they were taking. Instead of arriving back at the house, she found that they had reached the stable yard. Just beyond, in a white-fenced paddock, were four beautiful horses that immediately came cantering toward them. Forgetting her angry exchange with Garth, Nicola exclaimed in delight, "Oh, aren't they gorgeous!"

Garth looked on approvingly while she stroked the soft velvet muzzles that were thrust at her over the fence.

"There's not much call for horses on a sheep station these days," he observed. "We even use motorbikes or Land-Rovers for mustering. But to me it would seem all wrong to dispense with horses entirely. There's nothing like feeling a fine horse under you as you survey the countryside."

"Oh, I agree!" she said enthusiastically.

Garth gave her a thoughtful look. "Have you done much riding in England?"

"Not as much as I'd have liked," Nicola admitted ruefully. "For one reason or another, it wasn't always possible. But at the farm where I was last working they had a lovely little mare—it belonged to the farmer's daughter, but she had married and left home. So I was lucky, and I spent a lot of my spare time riding around on Ella."

"You'll enjoy a ride now, then! Which one do you fancy? I wouldn't advise the big stallion. Hector is inclined to be spirited."

Her keenness had betrayed her, Nicola realized in dismay. She tried to back down, but it was useless.

"Why pretend?" he said sternly. "You and I both know that you're absolutely longing for a ride. So for heaven's sake stop being childish."

"Just for a little while, then," she agreed weakly.

Garth let two of the horses out of the paddock and led them into the yard for saddling. For himself he'd chosen the big bay stallion, and for Nicola a frisky little chestnut mare named Kirstie, who seemed delighted at the prospect of an unexpected outing.

As they set off, taking a track that led westward toward the sinking sun, the starkly beautiful landscape glowed with flame and amber light, and the solitary gum trees were beginning to cast blue shadows. It was still very hot, but there was a slight stir of breeze—and, drifting on it, the subtle aromatic smell of grass and eucalyptus that Nicola had come to associate with the bush.

They must have ridden a couple of miles without speaking, the silence broken only by the soft thud of the horses' hooves on the dusty red earth. Then suddenly Garth said, "You ride extremely well, Nicola. You have poise and a natural sense of rhythm."

She made a deprecatory murmur, but she couldn't help feeling immensely flattered. After another silence Garth again spoke abruptly.

"What exactly is there between you and Tony?"

"I beg your pardon?" she said coldly, to gain time to consider her answer.

"You heard me."

"Yes, I heard. But I fail to understand how my

relationship with Tony can possibly be any concern of yours."

"So you admit that there *is* a relationship between you?"

Nicola bit her lip, cursing herself for using such an ill-chosen word. But she refused to be put on the defensive and merely shrugged her shoulders.

"I asked you a question, Nicola," he snapped, menace in his tone.

"And I've already given you the only answer you're going to get," she retorted.

With an impatient exclamation, Garth reined in his horse and stopped. Nicola would dearly have liked to ride on calmly, but the little mare followed suit and came to a halt beside the stallion.

"I suppose you realize," he went on, his craggy features set like stone, "that the two of you are being talked about?"

"Really? Then I'm happy to have done my bit in providing a topic for gossip," Nicola returned, her voice rather unsteady. "There must be a great dearth of excitement in the lives of the people hereabouts if they have to sink to discussing Tony and me."

Garth brushed that aside contemptuously. "They are saying," he persisted, "that it's all a little plot hatched by you and Angie—when she was with you in England, presumably—to provide a wife for her brother."

Nicola could have told him, quite simply and straightforwardly, that there was nothing beyond friendship between herself and Tony, and never would be. That Tony, despite being thoroughly pleasant and likable, just wasn't her sort of man when it came to physical attraction. But what gloating satisfaction that would give Garth! He would doubtless take the opportunity to remind her, humiliatingly, that by contrast he was very much her sort of man—in the physical sense. And she could hardly deny it. Even now, when he was throwing these hateful accusations at her, she was intensely aware of him, of his potent, smoldering virility.

She glanced away, gazing at the blue-hazed horizon. "And I suppose," she remarked sarcastically, "that Angie and I also arranged for Mrs. King to have a flare-up of her gallstones which necessitated an immediate operation, all so that I could be left alone at Dandaraga with Tony?"

"You needn't have been alone there with him if you hadn't chosen to," Garth pointed out harshly. "I gave you an alternative, and you refused it."

"Because it was totally unnecessary," she flashed. "It would have been absurd to uproot Mary Anstey for no good reason."

"Don't you mean," he suggested, giving her a bitter look, "that Mary would have been in the way?"

Nicola twitched the reins, hoping to end this conversation by moving on. But the mare refused to budge. It was as if, she thought wretchedly, Garth had cast a spell over the animal, rendering it powerless to move without his permission. Wearily, she tried another challenge.

"Why should it matter to you one way or the other what Tony and I feel about each other?"

Garth was silent, brushing a fly from his face with an impatient flick of his hand. When he finally answered, his voice was strangely subdued. "He's wrong for you, that's all."

"I'd have said that Tony has a lot going for him," she riposted. "But *you*, of course, couldn't be expected to understand his qualities—since they have nothing to do with ambition and greed. *You* would feel only contempt for a man who doesn't take it as his divine right to ride roughshod over anyone or anything that stands in his path."

"That's your judgment of me, is it?" he rapped.

"If the shoe fits!"

"Then how do you explain my concern over your relationship with Tony?"

Nicola felt quite reckless now. "Oh, very easily! It must upset your overinflated ego that a woman whom you've tried to seduce should be capable of turning to another man. In your opinion, I should be swooning at your feet, I suppose."

He gave a bark of incredulous laughter. "You seriously believe that I've tried to seduce you? Let me tell you this, pommie girl: if that had been my intention, then I would have succeeded."

"Really?" she exclaimed. "You've got a mighty big opinion of yourself."

"I state it as a simple fact," he returned blandly. "*I* know it's true, and *you* know it's true—however much you try to convince yourself otherwise."

"You're talking utter nonsense," she cried furiously. "You're the very last man on earth that I'd . . . I'd . . ."

"Why do you try to deny your own womanhood?" he demanded, his blue eyes burning into her. "It makes no more sense than for me to try to deny my manhood. Twice now I've proved emphatically that what I claim is true. Must I do so yet a third time before you're willing to acknowledge the fact?"

"You'll not get the opportunity," she flung at him angrily, and felt a shiver of dread run down her spine. "Not again, you won't!"

Garth made a sweeping gesure with his hand at the wide, empty space all around them. "Bold words, Nicola," he said ironically, "considering the position you happen to be in at the moment."

"You wouldn't dare!" she said, her mouth suddenly dry.

Garth's face tightened. "Have you learned nothing in your short life?" he inquired sarcastically. "It's a very risky thing to dare a man to prove himself."

"You would only succeed in proving yourself to be a callous, unfeeling lout," she responded, and somehow she made herself meet his eyes as she went on shakily, "But you've already done that, most successfully."

By the sheer force of his will he held her gaze captive, and Nicola felt like a hunted animal before a predator. She wanted desperately to look away but was powerless to do so. The expression on Garth's face was unreadable, his mouth set firm, his lean jaw clenched, his eyes slitted like ice chips. Was he furiously angry with her, or merely amused? Was he calculating whether or not to claim her with another of those possessive kisses that she had found so disturbing . . . a kiss this time intended as a preliminary to her total surrender? Was that why he had inveigled her to go riding with him, leading her to this lonely spot where there would be no one within call no matter how much she cried for help?

If this really was Garth's plan she would make him pay dearly for victory, she determined. He would have to drag her forcibly from her horse, and she would fight him like a wildcat. His handsome face, raked by her fingernails, would ever afterward bear witness to her frantic resistance.

From somewhere a treacherous voice rose up to question just how much, in truth, she would resist Garth's lovemaking. Just looking at him now, she felt herself go weak with the longing to be held again in his arms, to be kissed until she was dizzy with delight.

Then, abruptly, Garth glanced away, setting her free from his hypnotic gaze. Wheeling his horse, he started to canter back in the direction of the homestead. And humiliatingly, without any kind of command, her own mount followed meekly.

As they entered the stable yard, they heard a motorbike pull up by the gate. "Oh, good, here's Charley back," said Garth. "He can tell you if everything is okay at Dandaraga."

The motorbike rider cut the engine and propped up his machine before coming toward them. His dark skin was wizened and seamed, and Nicola realized that he was an Aborigine, a descendant of one of the first inhabitants of Australia.

"This is Miss Wyatt, Charley," introduced Garth.

"Ya, boss." It was not said rudely, but in the tone of a man being told what he already knew. He awarded Nicola a gap-toothed smile, knocking back his dusty brown muster hat with one thumb as a token of respect. "Your place is fine, missie, just dinkum fine. I put the chicks away safe from old man fox and fed the dogs."

"That's very good of you," she told him. "I hope you helped yourself to a beer while you were there."

He shook his head. "Nope! Never touch it, missie."

"I see. Well, thanks again."

A boy appeared from the stables, a cheerful, freckled lad of about fourteen whom Garth introduced as Micky, the son of one of his roustabouts, the men who worked the station. He took the horses, and Nicola was alone with Garth once again. As they strolled toward the house, Garth reminisced. "When I look back to my boyhood, I realize that Charley taught me a great deal of the ancient aboriginal wisdom. As a result, I expect I could survive in the open bush a lot better than most men . . . and out here, sheer survival is the name of the game if the trappings of civilization should fail you for any reason. I used to sit at Charley's feet—quite literally—and listen to him for hours on end."

Nicola tried to picture Garth as a boy, listening avidly to the old man's words of ancient lore and absorbing from him the primitive skills of his people. But it was hard to imagine Garth Rossiter as anything but the assertive, arrogantly self-confident man he had become.

"So now you keep Charley on as a sort of pensioner?" she said.

Garth shook his head. "Put that way, it implies the conscious granting and receiving of a favor, and it's not like that at all. He's his own man, Nicola . . . his own man!"

There was no evening coolness in the air yet, so why did she feel her skin prickling in a shiver?

"Is that something else you learned from Charley?" she asked. "How to be your own man?"

"Judge for yourself," he replied briefly, and ushered her up the veranda steps into the house.

Though Nicola had no change of clothes with her, she was glad to accept Garth's suggestion of a cool shower after their ride. The guest bathroom he showed her to was in complete contrast to the simple, utilitarian one at Dandaraga. Here there was an immaculate, gleaming tiled room with luxurious fittings. Water jetted copiously from the overhead spray, deliciously refreshing, with no hint that it should be used sparingly.

When Nicola emerged she noted from Garth's damp hair that he, too, had showered and had redonned the shirt and cotton drill trousers he had been wearing all day . . . presumably, she conceded, so as not to make her feel disheveled by comparison. It looked as if the man did have a few finer feelings, after all!

"A drink before we think of eating?" he suggested.

"Thank you. Er . . . I was wondering if you'd like me to prepare a meal, as Mary isn't here."

"Thanks for the offer, but there's no need," Garth told her as he poured a gin and tonic for himself and a glass of white wine for her. "Mary really spoils me, I'm afraid, and she's left a splendid cold collation ready which will be plenty for the two of us."

They sat on the veranda with their drinks in the fast-gathering dusk after sundown. Across the way, a light showed in the Ansteys' bungalow, and Nicola wished she could be in Jeff's friendly, easygoing company, rather than here with Garth. For a change he was being quite amiable, almost charming, yet she couldn't relax for an instant. She was constantly expecting an incautious word to spark off a return to the bitter antagonism between them. And worse still, she was disturbingly aware of his virile masculinity, which threatened to rob her of all common sense and decorum.

Time drifted by, every moment of it a sweet torment to her. At last, stretching his long frame luxuriously, Garth said, "Well, shall we go in and eat now?"

"If you like," Nicola shrugged, thankful to break the silent tension that had been building up between them. The kitchen, which blazed with light at the touch of a switch, was a large, bright room fitted with every imaginable piece of modern equipment. A serving cart was set ready, and Garth added to it extra plates and cutlery, and various platters and dishes he took from the fridge. Wheeling it through to the dining room, he didn't put the lights on there, but instead struck a match and lit two candles in silver candlesticks, which he placed on the oval mahogany table.

"So much more romantic like this," he remarked, and the pale candlelight, reflected in his eyes, was a mockery, even a threat. Nicola had half a mind to say that she would prefer more light on the scene, but to what end? Even if Garth acceded to her request he would still be the victor, having forced her to betray her fear of his insidious sensual attraction. No, she thought, steeling herself, let him try whatever seductive tricks he likes. He'll find that he can win no response from me but cool indifference.

They set the table between them. There was a large platter of cold turkey, ham, and tongue; also a bowl of green salad Garth had tossed with French dressing, and various other salad makings. To follow there was a selection of cheeses and crackers and a bowl of luscious-looking peaches. Garth opened a bottle of sparkling wine and poured it foaming into two tall glasses, which frosted over instantly with the icy coolness. He handed one to her, then raised his own in a toast.

"I'll drink to you, Nicola. May you learn wisdom before it's too late."

It was hardly a toast she could accept with equanimity. Recklessly, she raised her own glass, proclaiming loudly, "And I'll drink to you. May *you* learn humility before it's too late."

"Too late for what, I wonder?" he inquired interestedly, as he served some meat and handed her a plate.

Greatly to her surprise, Nicola found that the swim and the ride had made her quite hungry. In fact, she thoroughly enjoyed the meal.

"At least you have no inhibitions about eating," Garth remarked, as he poured the last of the wine into her glass.

"Do you find that reprehensible?" she flared quickly.

"Not at all. I greatly prefer an honest demonstration of appetite to self-denial through a fake sense of gentility. And that applies to *any* kind of appetite," he added meaningfully.

Draining her wine, Nicola toyed with the glass in her fingers, admiring the glinting cut crystal. She reflected that there was a certain pleasure in this verbal fencing with Garth.

"Judging from the amount of food Mary Anstey left for you," she said, with a little giggle, "you must normally eat like a horse."

Garth shrugged. "It seems to be a womanly instinct to overfeed a man. Not just his stomach, but his vanity too. I think that in some ways Mary sees me as the son she never had."

"Your vanity doesn't need any feeding," Nicola riposted, and felt rather pleased with herself.

"Is that why you constantly splash on an astringent antidote?" He laughed and rose to his feet. "Let's have coffee in the lounge, shall we? Mary will have left it all ready in the percolator."

As she rose to follow him Nicola felt a slight—and pleasurable—muzziness. Her reckless mood continuing, she said teasingly, "Does Mary run your bath and lay out your clothes for you, too?"

Garth stopped in the doorway and turned to face her so suddenly that Nicola bumped into him. She stepped back hastily, but not before the impact with his lean masculine body had sent a tingling response running through her.

"Would *you* run my bath and lay out my clothes for me, Nicola?" he asked in a caressing voice.

She was still shaken, still trembling from the physical contact. But she forced a flip response. "I can't think of any circumstances in which I'd be called upon to do so," she said.

"Use your imagination," he said softly, holding her gaze.

Nicola wrenched her eyes away. Using her imagination, letting it have free rein, would be all too easy—but it was something she must fight against with all her strength! Covertly, she watched Garth from behind her dark lashes as he attended to the coffee. As he bent forward, his shirt was stretched tautly across his broad back and the contours of his sinewy muscles were clearly defined. Again she felt that insane but almost irresistible urge to touch him, to stroke the skin at the back of his neck and tangle her fingers into that fair, sun-bleached hair.

In a frantic effort to distract her rebellious thoughts and lead the conversation into safer channels, she decided to attack Garth on the question of Tony.

"I suppose you must be delighted," she said, taking a seat on the large green velvet sofa, "that Tony is faced with a heavy repair bill for his utility truck."

Garth glanced at her over his shoulder. "Why should I be delighted at someone else's misfortune?"

"Because the deeper Tony gets into the red, the more vulnerable he becomes to you!"

There was a brief silence; then Garth said, in a voice that held anger in check, "It's not *my* fault he's in the red, you know."

"Maybe not, but you gloat over it. And it's not poor Tony's fault, either."

"That," Garth replied, "is arguable. But whatever the state of Tony's finances, it's highly irresponsible of him not to have reliable transport in this sort of territory. If not for Jeff, all the machinery at Dandaraga would have packed up long ago."

"I suppose you begrudge Jeff giving a helping hand," Nicola flung at him.

"Why should I? As long as Jeff does a good job for me—which he certainly does—then how he spends the rest of his time is entirely up to him. But it might have been better for Tony if Jeff hadn't always been so ready to put right everything that goes wrong with Tony's vehicles and so on. Then Tony would have been forced to equip himself properly."

"What with?" Nicola demanded bitterly. "What's he supposed to use for money?"

"I hardly think this is the time or place for a long lecture on the economics of sheep rearing in the outback," said Garth as he handed Nicola her cup of coffee and took a seat beside her. "In a nutshell, though, Tony's land is appallingly underutilized, which amounts to criminal negligence in my view. In his father's time they employed three or four men at Dandaraga and the place thrived. But in these days, when labor costs so much more—and rightly so—cost-efficiency is what it's all about. Tony Carson's land is superior to any that I've got here, and consequently ought to support a proportionately higher population of sheep, acre for acre. But it doesn't. The biggest enemy in the bush, as you'll have seen for yourself, is the shortage of water. Yet Tony would have plenty, if only he'd drill for it."

"With his bare hands, I suppose?" she retorted sarcastically. "Sinking an artesian well costs money, remember. So poor Tony had to stand by and watch you drilling right up close to his boundary, and then piping a trickle of the yield across to him as a sop to your conscience."

"More than a trickle," Garth corrected sharply. "But I'm surprised that you grant me a conscience at

104

all, Nicola. I thought I was supposed to have a heart of stone."

She ignored the gibe. "It's ridiculous, your trying to make out that it's Tony's fault he's in debt to the bank. He works like a slave, and nobody could suggest that he's a spendthrift. He hasn't got extravagant personal tastes, and he doesn't possess a single thing that could be classed as a luxury."

"Agreed! But the profits—such as they are—have been frittered away over the years through sheer bad management and neglect. For instance, he's allowed the quality of his wool clip to deteriorate because he wouldn't pay out for top breeding rams to serve his ewes. Many's the time I've urged Tony to take a different course of action in one way or another, but he never listens."

"He'd be a fool to listen to *you*," Nicola broke in scornfully, "considering that your aim is to get your grasping hands on his land."

Garth sighed impatiently. "If Tony was sensible he'd take my money—it's more than Dandaraga is worth, incidentally, considering the debts he would leave behind—and buy himself a market-garden smallholding. A few acres on the Gawler River near Adelaide or somewhere would suit him nicely."

"And get him nicely out of your way," Nicola tacked on. But she had an uneasy thought that there might be something in what Garth said. She had often noticed how Tony could hardly wait to get home from the paddocks to work on his struggling vegetable patch. Her niggling doubts made her speak all the more vehemently as she demanded, "Why don't you leave Tony alone?"

"You mean, leave him to rot?" Garth suggested. "What does Angie think, I wonder. Has she talked to you about it?"

"Well, Angie's not so keen on the sheep station as he is," Nicola confessed. "She admits that she's really a city girl at heart. But she feels that she can't let Tony down by going off and leaving him to cope alone."

Garth's eyes glittered. "And that's the reason you're here, of course, to replace Angie. Only you'd be rather more than a replacement for a sister!" Quite suddenly his voice changed from being sarcastic, and there was a note almost of pleading. "You mustn't do it, Nicola, you really mustn't."

His switch to gentleness was her undoing, and Nicola felt her eyes fill with unbidden tears. Unable to answer Garth for the thickness in her throat, she shook her head from side to side in protest, though she didn't know quite what she meant. In the muted light of a single shaded table lamp, his face was somber, its leanness etched with deep shadows. He reached for her, and slowly, as if in a dream, she let him gather her into his arms. He pressed his lips to her hair, then touched a trail of tingling kisses across her cheek and finally found her mouth. This time there was no brutal demand, no arrogant assertion of his masculinity. His clasp upon her was tender, almost reverent. She was no longer afraid of his strength, but reveled in the iron-strong band of his encircling arms, which, if he had a will to, could crush her slender body so easily.

"Oh, Nicola," he murmured and kissed her once more, long and lingeringly.

Again Nicola experienced the strange, wondrous feeling of isolation . . . just herself and Garth alone in all the universe. Every other thought was driven from her mind as the seconds slipped away, the minutes running one into another until the passing of time had no meaning. It was just she and Garth, his hands caressing the soft, yielding contours of her body, hers stroking the lean muscularity of his. Their murmured sighs and whispered words were only breath-loud in the pervading silence, softer than the mingled beating of their two hearts. Floating on a rosy cloud of rapture, she became aware of the growing urgency of Garth's desire. And still she clung to him, wanting only that this sweet ecstasy of sensual delight should never end.

He raised his head slightly to look down at her, and in the softly shaded lamplight his eyes seemed dark and smoldering. When he spoke, his voice was husky and resonant, coming from deep within his throat.

"Nicola, you're so beautiful, so very beautiful. Oh, Nicola . . ."

"Garth," she whispered back, loving the very sound of his name that seemed to echo and reecho in the stillness of the room.

His fingers began to undo the buttons of her shirt, and it was then that Nicola felt the first stirrings of unease.

"No!" she protested weakly, unwilling even now to bring a note of discord into the blissful sense of oneness they had so miraculously achieved.

"Yes," he persisted, his hand slipping in to the fastening of her bra. The next instant, to Nicola's dismay, he had undone the clasp and she felt her breasts fall loose.

"No!" she cried again, sharply and shrilly, tensing in every limb.

"You can't back down now," Garth muttered, a new note of harshness in his voice. "Not this time!"

Full awareness of what was happening reached through to Nicola like a great gushing torrent of ice-cold water. So this was all it was, all it had ever been to Garth—a crude seduction! Ringing in her ears was a bitter echo of his cruel gibe when they were out riding in the bush, his statement that she would find herself a helpless victim in his arms. And he had so nearly proved it to be true.

Her hatred of him came surging back, choking her with its intensity, and she tried to thrust herself away in a desperate effort to get free. But Garth refused to let her escape. He fought her without mercy, demonstrating with what contemptuous ease he could restrain her.

Stricken with panic, Nicola wondered if he intended to subdue her by force.

Then suddenly Garth let her go and rose to his feet. He stood staring down at her with eyes that glinted fury and scorn. "Have it your way, then!" he gritted. "Your sort of woman wants to have her cake and eat it, too. I suppose you enjoy all this? Well, don't worry; as we both know, you're hardly my only choice in women. Or even my first!"

Wretchedly, Nicola sat up and drew together her unbuttoned shirt to conceal her nakedness. "It's hateful of you to throw that in my face," she sobbed, somehow forcing out the words through the thickness of her tears. "How you must delight in your power over us! Do you notch up each conquest as yet another triumph for your incredible self-conceit?"

Standing over her, the muscles of his tight-clenched jaw working with fury, he looked a dark, menacing figure. "Don't worry," he rasped. "Nothing happened. And nothing will happen, not now. So you can cling safely to your frozen virtue. It won't be threatened by me, pommie girl—not if you were to come begging on your hands and knees."

Nicola gasped in outrage. "Do you imagine that I ever want to set eyes on you again?" she cried. "I despise you utterly, Garth Rossiter, and everything you stand for. You're a bully and a liar and a cheat, and I fervently hope that one day you meet the fate you deserve." Seizing the chance to drive the knife still deeper, she went on recklessly. "But then, your fate is already settled, isn't it? Zoe Drysdale and you are just about right for each other, I'd say . . . two utterly selfish people who happily trample on anyone who has the impertinence to stand up to them—"

"That's enough!" he snarled. "You'd better hold your tongue, my girl, or I might . . ."

"You might do what?" she taunted him. "Perhaps you'd like to hit me and prove that you're a brute as well as everything else?"

108

"That's enough, I said!" His voice cut across her like a whiplash, and his face was thunderous.

"If . . . if you have the smallest grain of decency in you," Nicola faltered wretchedly, "you'll clear out of this room and give me a few minutes to . . . to tidy myself. I won't be long, I promise you, because every moment I remain in your house I feel more contaminated. As soon as I'm ready I'll go outside and wait there for Mary to get home."

With a savage exclamation of rage Garth turned and went to the door. "You can stay where you are for as long as you like! You'll have the whole bloody house to yourself, because I'm going out to get some fresh air. I need it!"

Chapter Six

"It's Tony!" said Nicola excitedly to Mary Anstey, when she saw the dusty utility truck approaching. "Oh, that's wonderful! He's much earlier than I was expecting."

The two women were sitting together on the Ansteys' shady veranda enjoying a cup of coffee. The first part of the morning had been taken up by Mary's bubbling account of her visit to her daughter's and how well her first grandchild was progressing and what an absolute little darling he was. And there were numerous snapshots to prove it. Later, she had taken Nicola around and introduced her to the wives of the station hands employed at Kuranda. They all seemed very friendly and more than happy for the chance of a chat with someone new.

Of Garth she had seen nothing beyond a glimpse across the yard, when they had exchanged freezing nods. But he, too, must have heard the approach of Tony's truck, for at that minute he emerged from one of the outbuildings to see who the new arrival was.

Nicola couldn't have said precisely what motivated her to run and greet Tony quite so enthusiastically. She really was glad to see him, naturally . . . and immensely relieved that her sojourn at Garth's place was being brought to an end some hours earlier than she'd thought possible. But she was also very aware that

Garth was watching her as she ran forward across the yard.

"It's great to see you, Tony!" she exclaimed eagerly, giving him a radiant welcoming smile. "How marvelous that you got the truck fixed so quickly."

Looking highly gratified, Tony climbed from the driver's seat and took both her hands in his. "You're a sight for sore eyes, Nikki, and no mistake!" The way he looked at her, so fondly, so tenderly, made Nicola feel embarrassed. But she defiantly refused to break away from Tony while Garth was observing them.

"Come and have some coffee with Mary and me," she invited. She let him retain hold of one of her hands as they walked back to the veranda.

"I really hustled Sam at the garage," Tony explained, "and he started work on my clutch at six A.M. I was so impatient to get back to you, Nikki. I really hated having to let you go off with Garth like that yesterday, but what else could I do?"

"It didn't matter," she told him. Feeling that it was quite unnecessary to go into details about Mary's not getting home until midnight, she added, "The Ansteys are really super people, Tony, and they've made me feel thoroughly welcome."

Mary suggested that Tony might prefer a cool beer to coffee after his dusty drive, and while he was drinking this Garth came strolling over. Nicola could feel the leaden weight of his gaze, even though he didn't look at her directly.

"You got your truck fixed okay, then?" he said to Tony.

"Yep!" Tony pulled a long face. "It cost me a packet, though."

Garth nodded brusquely. "It's cheaper in the long run to keep your transport well maintained. And safer. One of these days you'll have a breakdown way out in the bush and then you'll be in real trouble."

Tony grunted but said nothing. It wasn't until they

had set off, after Nicola had given profuse thanks to Mary Anstey and received a pressing invitation from her to come and visit as often as she liked, that Tony let his anger show.

"That bloody man!" he exclaimed furiously. "How dare he speak to me as if I were just a kid still wet behind the ears?"

"I agree, he's quite insufferable," Nicola said vehemently.

Tony shot her a sideways look. "I'm glad you understand that, Nikki! A fellow like Garth can switch the charm on with girls, and . . ."

"Not with me!" she said, shuddering.

It seemed to Nicola that Tony digested her fierce reaction to Garth with a certain amount of satisfaction. After a couple of minutes' silence, he said, "I phoned Angie at her hotel last night. We had quite a chat."

"Is everything okay?" Nicola asked quickly. "Aunt Janet is still making good progress?"

"Oh, sure, Aunt Janet's just fine!" He paused again, then remarked with a nervous laugh, "But if I know anything about that sis of mine, there's something going on."

"How do you mean, Tony?"

"Well, I reckon all that about wanting to stay on at Broken Hill to keep Aunt Janet company is only half the story," he said thoughtfully. "From one or two slight hints she let drop, it looks to me as if there's a man in the picture."

"You mean someone she's met at Broken Hill?"

Tony nodded. "She kept going on about a fellow who was a patient in the hospital there with a splintered kneecap—a mining engineer by the name of Barry Mitchell. He's just been discharged now, apparently, and as he can't drive himself yet Angie said she's been chauffeuring him around a bit this last day or two." He glanced at Nicola again. "I reckon it's serious."

"Good for her!" she said, pleased. "Angie deserves someone nice."

Tony was silent, as if brooding, and Nicola could guess why. Although he would be happy for his sister and anxious not to stand in her way, the prospect of Angie's getting married placed him in an awkward position. Would he be able to keep going at Dandaraga station without her help?

After a moment Tony said with a forced laugh, "Don't we all?"

"Don't we all what?"

"Deserve someone nice."

His hand drifted down from the steering wheel and came to rest on Nicola's where it lay on the seat. Her first instinct was to pull away; clearly Tony's ideas about her were becoming too positive. But something made her hesitate . . . a sort of defiance against the man who had so nearly succeeded in seducing her last night. If she could let herself feel something for Tony, wouldn't it go to prove that she felt nothing for Garth except anger and disgust? So she allowed her hand to remain where it was until Tony had to use the gearshift. Then, as if casually, she moved in her seat and placed her hand where it was well out of his reach.

When they arrived at Dandaraga they found Charley in the yard, tossing corn to the chickens. The two dogs appeared from nowhere, bounding forward to greet them with welcoming barks. Nicola stooped to pat them while Tony walked over to the old man.

"Thanks for coming, Charley," she heard him say. "I understand you were here yesterday, too." Tony dipped a hand into his pocket for his wallet. "Er . . . can I give you something for your trouble?"

The grizzled head nodded emphatically. "You surely can, Mr. Carson." Nicola felt a swift stab of disappointment, but then the old man added with a dry chuckle, "How about making it a handshake? That be fair, you reckon, Mr. Carson?"

"Oh, but I think I ought . . ." The gnarled old hand was extended to him, and Tony took it with an awkward laugh. "Well, if you really mean it, Charley . . . thanks a lot!"

As the old man departed on his motorbike in a burst of noise and a cloud of dust, Tony grumbled, "He's an independent blighter."

"Oh, no!" Nicola protested. "I thought his attitude was rather touching."

Tony shrugged and gave a rueful laugh. "I suppose I do tend to feel lemony about everyone from Kuranda."

"Surely not Jeff and Mary?"

"That's true. I'd have been a darn sight more unhappy about you flying back to Kuranda with Garth yesterday if I hadn't known that you'd be staying over with them." He glanced at her questioningly. "I suppose you didn't see much of Garth after you landed?"

Nicola cursed the way hot color flamed her face. "Well, actually . . . as a matter of fact, I did have a meal with him," she admitted reluctantly. "You see, it turned out that Mary was away visiting her married daughter and she wasn't due back until late, so . . . well, I couldn't very well install myself in their house in Mary's absence, could I, without her even knowing that I was coming?"

"Blast!" said Tony explosively. "I wouldn't mind betting that Garth had it all worked out, curse him! When exactly did Mary get back?"

"Oh . . . ." She tried to make it sound unimportant. "It was around midnight, I think."

"And you were with Garth all that time?" Tony took a quick breath and asked, "Did he try anything on, Nikki?"

"Try anything on?" she echoed.

"Well, you know what I mean . . . did he make a pass at you?"

Nicola felt like bursting into tears. Instead she managed to say with a forced laugh, "Nothing that I couldn't handle."

"So he did make a play for you!" Tony scowled

blackly. "It doesn't surprise me one bit. To Garth, every woman is a challenge; he wants to see how fast he can get her into bed."

"Well, he didn't succeed with me," she cried, feeling waves of pain wash over her at the humiliating memory of how near she had come to being just another conquest of Garth Rossiter's. In her wretchedness, she hit back at Tony. "I'll remind you that I never wanted to go to Kuranda with Garth when your truck broke down. But you insisted."

"I know, I know, it was all my fault," Tony acknowledged unhappily. "But it seemed the most sensible plan at the time. I hated the thought of you spending a dismal evening alone in the hotel at Boolaroo."

"It would have been infinitely preferable," Nicola retorted before she could check herself. The remark brought a curious look from Tony. She guessed that he wanted to question her further but was too scared of the angry response he would get from her.

"Come on, let's go inside and get something to eat," he suggested after a moment. "I could just do with one of your super meals. You're a marvelous cook, Nikki."

She shrugged. "I'm fairly ordinary, really."

Tony's eyes became tender. "Nothing about you is ordinary," he said softly. "You're a very special girl."

Nicola was thankful to go inside and occupy herself in the kitchen. She scratched up a hasty dinner of ham and eggs and peas, with canned pears and ice cream to follow, and the usual large pot of tea. And afterward they had to get busy catching up on the work that had been neglected. Taking with them a large vacuum flask of more tea and some wedges of a fruitcake she had baked a few days before, they remained out in the paddocks until the light began to fail. When they finally returned to the homestead it was already quite dark.

Nicola showered first, and when Tony had showered and changed he joined her in the kitchen, where she was grilling chops.

"Let's have a bottle of wine with the meal," he suggested.

Nicola glanced around at him in surprise. "Why? What's special about this evening?" she asked.

Tony gave a quick, nervous laugh. "If you don't know already, Nikki, you'll soon find out."

She sighed inwardly, realizing that tonight she had another battle on her hands . . . a very different sort of battle. Yesterday she had faced an experienced womanizer who, in addition to his own selfish gratification, wanted to force an abject admission from her that she couldn't resist his lovemaking. Lovemaking! To use that phrase about the arrogant, self-centered Garth Rossiter made an utter mockery of something that should be beautiful and precious. Now this evening, with Tony, she had to deal with a gentle, kind man who sincerely imagined that he was falling in love with her . . . a man she could respect as she could never respect Garth Rossiter. Yet she knew instinctively that Tony could never evoke those rapturous stirrings of her body as Garth had done with such expert ease.

In a way, Nicola wished that it *could* happen for her with Tony. She could imagine life with him here in the outback . . . a hard struggle, yes, but infinitely worthwhile and rewarding. Working together, they would surely be able to make Dandaraga thrive somehow, despite all that Garth might do to cause problems for them.

Alas, though, she feared that she could never feel more for Tony than a deep fondness. Was she spoiled for any decent man? she wondered wretchedly, now that she had met Garth, now that he had shown her what magic could flow between man and woman?

After supper they washed up together, then Nicola made coffee and took it through to the living room. Tony was fiddling with the radio, trying to tune out the static that marred the music.

"Storm's brewing somewhere," he commented as he came to sit beside her on the sofa. Nicola wished that

116

she'd chosen an armchair, but to move now would be too obvious.

Tony cleared his throat, hemmed and hawed for a minute, then burst out, "You and me, Nikki . . . we get on pretty well, right?"

"Of course we do," she said nervously.

He reached over and took hold of her hand. "I bet we could make a go of it; don't you?"

Nicola bit her lip, looking at him with troubled eyes. "Tony, you mustn't let your imagination run away with you. I mean, it's just the way things have happened, that's all . . . Aunt Janet needing the operation and Angie going with her and leaving us alone here. The point is, it could have been any girl. . . ."

"Oh, no, that's not true, Nikki," he protested. "I knew almost from the moment I first saw you that you were the girl for me. Honestly, you've got to believe that."

"I . . . I know that you like me . . ." she began carefully.

"*Like* you!" he exclaimed. "I'm in love with you, Nikki."

"No!" She tried to draw her hand gently away, but his grip was too tight. "You . . . you only think you are, Tony, because you're lonely and worried."

"I wouldn't be lonely if I had you, Nikki. Say that you like me, just a little bit."

"Of course I do. I like you very much."

"Well, then . . . !"

"Liking isn't the same thing as loving," she pointed out in a quiet voice.

"But it *could* be, if only you'd let yourself," he argued. "Don't keep me at a distance, Nikki . . . I want to hold you in my arms and kiss you."

"No," she said. "No, you mustn't."

"Please," he begged and reached out for her. She held back momentarily, but she was melted by the look of pleading in his hazel eyes. Poor Tony; life had handed him a pretty rough deal. If she could bring him a little happiness, what did a few kisses matter? They might even serve to bring her a certain comfort, easing the terrible heartache she felt.

So she nodded, smiling at him, and Tony gathered her into his arms with a murmur of thankfulness. His lips were cool, soft, and undemanding . . . so utterly different from Garth's harsh and passionate possession of her mouth. Was this, after all, what love *should* be?

Tony let her go and breathed a sigh of deep contentment. "Oh, Nikki, I do love you . . . truly I do. I could make you happy, I'm sure I could. And it's obvious that you have a real affinity for life on the land."

"That's true," she admitted. "But . . . but . . ."

"Is it the outback?" he inquired anxiously. "Are you scared at the thought of being so isolated here?"

"No, I think the outback is beautiful. There's something very real and basic about it, something deeply satisfying. But—"

"Then let's get married," Tony broke in, his eyes glowing.

"No," she protested quickly.

"I'm sorry, Nikki darling," he apologized. "Have I rushed you too much? It's just . . . well, I can't bear the thought of losing you, of you going back to England."

"But I've got to go back, Tony," she said sadly. "Right away. I can't marry you . . . surely you can see that?"

Tony looked at her beseechingly. "Don't say it, Nikki, please! At least, stay on here for as long as you originally planned. I'm sure that if you do, you'll come to see me in a different light. If you can't quite bring yourself to say yes to marrying me, then don't say no either. Give me a chance, that's all I ask."

Riven with doubt, Nicola hesitated, and that was fatal. The next moment she found herself agreeing to his plea. Yes, she would remain for the full two months arranged with Angie, and if by the end of that time . . .

"But I'm promising nothing, Tony," she warned him. "You do understand that?"

She had committed herself to staying on, that was all, but she was scared. Listening to Tony expounding on plans for the future development of Dandaraga station—plans that included her in every breath—she realized how difficult she had made it for herself to break free from him when the time came.

Perhaps, after all, she thought forlornly, things would work out for the best. Perhaps, if she tried hard enough, it was possible to *make* oneself fall in love with someone. And another perhaps—an even bigger one—was that she could somehow dispel those haunting memories of Garth that constantly tormented her.

Next morning, as usual, Nicola left Tony in the paddocks and returned to the homestead to prepare the substantial midday dinner. She was in the middle of making pastry when she heard a car draw up outside. Oh, no! she groaned inwardly, not Garth! That was just too cruel. She still felt far too shattered by what had happened between them to face him again with any degree of composure.

But it was not Garth. While she stood hesitating, she heard a female voice caroling, "Anyone at home?"

Zoe! What on earth did *she* want, calling like this out of the blue?

"Hallo, Zoe," she said rather ungraciously as she pushed open the screen door.

"Nicola! I'm so glad to have caught you in." The magnificent green eyes glinted with derisive amusement at the sight of Nicola's floury hands and the homely cotton apron she was wearing. "My word, aren't we getting domesticated?"

Nicola let that pass. "Did you want to see Tony?"

"Not especially! I . . . er, I was just passing, and I thought I'd drop in for a chat."

That was obviously a lie, but Nicola pretended to

accept it at its face value. "How was your trip to Sydney?" she inquired with false pleasantry.

"Oh, great! It's not a bad city, you know. You ought to get Tony to take you there sometime."

"I doubt if there will be any opportunity," Nicola replied coolly, thinking that even the week she'd been planning to spend in Sydney with Angie before she returned to England was probably out now.

"If only you can knock a bit of sense into Tony's head," Zoe persisted, "he'd have the time and the money to enjoy himself, and—"

Nicola cut across her. "I'm sorry, but I don't feel I have any right to be discussing Tony's business."

"You could make it your business, too," Zoe responded, with a meaningful smile. "Drop Tony a hint that if he were to twist Garth's arm he could get the offer for Dandaraga increased." Her smile deepened into a conspiratorial between-us-women look. "I'd see to that, you can count on it."

Trapped into indiscretion, Nicola said, "I understood that Garth's present offer was considerably above the market price."

"It is, sweetie! But what's money, when you've got loads? Take my word for it, you and Tony could line your pockets very nicely if you set about it the right way."

"It's entirely Tony's affair and nothing to do with me."

"No?" Zoe gave a silvery, tinkling laugh. "But that's only a matter of time, isn't it?"

About to deny the suggestion forcefully, Nicola checked herself. Why worry what Zoe Drysdale chose to think about the situation between herself and Tony? So she merely lifted her shoulders in an enigmatic shrug.

Zoe was watching her intently, seeming puzzled. The smile remained fixed on her face, but the green eyes narrowed to jealous pinpoints.

"I gather that Tony's truck had a breakdown in

Boolaroo and that Garth flew you back to Kuranda with him."

"That's right," agreed Nicola in an even tone. "I stayed overnight with the Ansteys, and Tony collected me from their place yesterday morning."

"Oh, I see; that's how it was." Nicola noticed the flicker of relief pass across her beautiful features. So in telling Zoe about the episode, she reflected, Garth must have been vague about the details of just where she had slept. And that was the reason for Zoe's coming here this morning . . . to check up on her—and on him!

Nicola suddenly felt in a reckless mood and regretted having rushed in with a reassuring account of where she'd spent the night at Kuranda station. Why shouldn't the suave, superior Zoe Drysdale be made to suffer a little?

"If you're staying, I'm afraid you'll have to excuse the kitchen, Zoe. I've got an apple pie that I must get into the oven." Nicola led the way inside, and as she began rolling out the pastry she went on in a chatty tone. "It was a bit awkward at Kuranda, actually, because when Garth and I arrived there we discovered that Mary was away visiting her married daughter. I couldn't very well just land myself on Jeff for the entire evening, so . . ." She paused a moment for emphasis. "So Garth kept me company."

Zoe's poise was clearly shaken. "What do you mean, 'kept you company'?" she demanded suspiciously.

"Oh, we swam and went riding. And then . . . well, we served up the meal Mary had left ready for him and dined together . . . just the two of us."

"What . . . what time did Mary get back?" Zoe asked in a low voice.

"Oh, very late. Sometime around midnight, I think it was. Not before."

In any other circumstances the expression of jealous fury on Zoe's face would have been highly gratifying. But Nicola found she could get no kind of pleasure or satisfaction from using Garth's loathsome attempt at seduction as a tactical weapon against Zoe. Feeling sickened and ashamed, she tried to make reparations by adding quickly, "Nothing happened, you know."

"Nothing happened?" It was clear that Zoe didn't believe her. Doubtless she knew Garth well enough to realize that he would be incapable of spending an entire evening alone in the company of a reasonably attractive girl without trying to chalk up another conquest. And, with his devastating charm, as likely as not succeeding, Nicola thought bitterly. She felt her cheeks flaming as she reflected what a very narrow escape it had been.

Fortunately, Tony arrived home at this juncture, so there was no chance of any further conversation between the two women. Tony didn't look any too pleased at discovering Zoe there, and Nicola had a feeling that he found her smooth sophistication rather overwhelming. But he repaired Nicola's omission of hospitality by going to the fridge and taking out some cans of beer.

"How about a lager?" he suggested.

Zoe accepted condescendingly, as if she were doing him a favor. Nicola asked for iced tea, and he poured the three glasses and brought them over. Taking a hasty sip, Nicola continued with her interrupted preparations for dinner. She felt horribly self-conscious as she bustled around putting the finishing touches to the meal under Zoe's supercilious gaze.

"Hey, Tony, you've got a good cook there!" she said with a soft laugh.

"Don't I know it!" he agreed warmly. "But then, Nikki's good at everything she handles. She's a great girl."

Zoe's eyes flickered from one to the other of them. It was as if she was gauging the exact state of their relationship. Eventually, she said in a lazy drawl, "You'll be sorry, I expect, when Angie and your aunt come home from Broken Hill."

"Why should we be?" demanded Nicola quickly, before Tony could say anything.

The green eyes danced derisively. "You two have a very cozy little setup here, haven't you? Are you going to make it legal?"

This time it was Tony who got in first. His answer seemed directed more at Nicola than at Zoe. "That's what I long for most in all the world," he said, deep feeling in his voice.

At once Zoe seemed in a more cheerful mood. "Then let me play the good fairy," she said jokingly, and snatched up a wooden spoon from where Nicola had left it on the scrubbed kitchen table. "See, I'll wave my magic wand and weave a spell over you. There, now; that has ensured that all your lovely dreams will come true. Bless you, my children!" Giving Nicola a very direct glance, she added, "And don't forget what I told you. It's good advice!"

She took another sip of lager, as if drinking their health, then put the glass down still half full. "Well, now, I must be off." On her way to the door, she paused and glanced back. "I've just had a great idea! How about you two coming over for dinner one evening? Say, tomorrow?"

Nicola longed for Tony to make some excuse and refuse the invitation. Instead, he just looked puzzled. "What's this in aid of, Zoe?"

She pouted at him prettily. "Does a dinner invite always have to be in aid of something? Still, if you like, let's say it's by way of being a little celebration."

"A celebration of what?" he asked.

"Of the magic spell I've just woven, of course," she replied gaily. "In the absence of anyone else, you need somebody to say 'Congratulations and blessings.'"

"No!" Nicola cried out instinctively, but too late. Zoe had already skipped out and across the hall. Tony followed her outside, and Nicola could hear them talking. She should have run out herself and put a stop to this ridiculous nonsense, but her legs felt too shaky to move.

She heard Zoe's car drive off; then Tony returned, a gratified smirk on his face. "Well, I must say that was unexpected," he remarked thoughtfully. "I've never been invited to the Drysdales' before, except to one of their big parties. We *are* honored!"

"Tony, we can't possibly go," Nicola protested.

"Why not?" he said mildly. "Although there's plenty I don't like about Zoe, she does seem to be putting herself out to be pleasant this time."

Nicola almost stamped her foot in fury. "Can't you see what she's up to?"

"Up to?" Tony stared. "How do you mean, Nikki?"

"It's all part of the plan to drive you out of Dandaraga . . ." she began, and then stopped. How could she possibly explain to Tony without repeating the conversation that had taken place between herself and Zoe?

Tony was looking puzzled. "I can't see that inviting us to dinner will help her do that," he argued. "By the way, what was it Zoe said to you about not forgetting her good advice?"

"Oh . . . nothing!" Nicola turned away quickly and started straining the potatoes.

Tony came to stand beside her. "It must have been *something*, Nikki," he persisted. "Was it about us . . . you and me?"

The saucepan went down into the sink with a clatter, and Nicola swung around to face him. "If you must know, it was about you selling this place to Garth. Zoe said she was certain that if you twisted his arm he'd up his offer for Dandaraga by quite a lot. That," she added chokily, "just shows how disloyal Zoe is to . . . to the man she's going to marry."

Tony's face was a study of perplexity. "But why should she tell *you* that, Nikki?"

"To get rid of me . . . of *us*," she amended hastily.

"Zoe has got the idea in her head that if you were to be offered a good price for Dandaraga, there'd be enough for . . . for us to get married on." Nicola said it boldly, though her lower lip quivered. "Only it's just not on, Tony. . . . I mean, irrespective of whether or not you should sell this place, I could never marry you. She's got it all wrong!"

A whole varity of expressions had flitted across Tony's face, but he ended up by giving her a reproachful look. "You promised me that you'd keep an open mind about that," he reminded her. "You promised you wouldn't give me a definite turndown until you'd thought about it some more."

"I know I did," she said miserably. "But . . ."

He touched her arm in quick protest. "No, Nikki, I'm not listening to you . . . not for a long while yet. Let's just carry on as we are for a bit and see how things go. I still think I can persuade you to change your mind, if you'll just give me the chance."

Nicola heaved a deep, unhappy sigh. If only, she thought desperately, she could be whisked off on some magic carpet, far away from her nightmare problems. But there was no place on earth so far distant that memories would not continue to haunt her. Torturing memories of Garth . . . the deliriously sweet sensation of his lips upon hers and his strong arms crushing her against his magnificently virile body.

With frantic determination she thrust such thoughts to the outermost edges of her mind. "Okay, then, Tony, I'll do as you ask and leave things for a while longer. But meantime you must promise me that you won't be tempted to sell out to Garth. Don't be tricked by him into selling your birthright and letting him win by the sheer power of his wretched money."

Tony regarded her doubtfully. "That all seems relatively unimportant now. If only I could feel confident of providing enough to make you happy, Nikki, I'd struggle on here forever trying to make a go of things. But if not . . . don't you see? You're far more important to me than any piece of land. And if staying on at Dandaraga is going to mean a life of near-poverty for you, then I'd prefer to get out and try something else . . . anything!"

Nicola would have liked to declare passionately that she would be happy to face poverty and worse for the sake of the man she loved. But she didn't love Tony . . . she never *could* love Tony. She knew now that, however long she let things drift between them, her answer would always have to be no.

In a husky voice she muttered, "I'm wrong to interfere, Tony. The decision must be yours, and yours alone."

"I want it to be *ours,* Nikki. Our decision."

"But it can't be, don't you see . . . ?"

Tony was shaking his head at her, reproachful once more. "We'll leave it for now . . . hold everything over, as you promised. Later on . . . well, then will be the time to decide what's to be done. I'll wait, Nikki, for as long as you want me to wait. I love you, you see."

"Don't say that," she begged. "It's not fair, Tony."

"But it's true! I do love you, and you can't stop me loving you."

But would he still love her, she thought desolately, if he had any idea of what had taken place between her and Garth at the Kuranda homestead? As a man who believed in decency and morality, Tony would be horrified to know how close she had come to behaving like a wanton the other night. How, even now, every nerve of her body cried out for the ultimate ecstasy of being possessed by Garth Rossiter—a despicable man whom she despised utterly.

Dinner was a moody meal, each of them locked away in private thoughts. Afterward, while Nicola washed the dishes, Tony went off to knock a nail into a loose post on the veranda. Wretchedly, she pondered about the following evening . . . they were committed now and would have to go to the Drysdales'. Suddenly a new thought darted into her head. Would Garth be there, too? Almost certainly, she told herself with a heart-stabbing pain. A dinner plate slipped from her fingers and fell to the floor with a crash.

Chapter Seven

Seen close to, the Drysdale homestead was even grander than it had appeared when seen from the air. Most unusually for the outback, it was two stories high, and it looked like some old colonial mansion of the nineteenth century. Nevertheless, it was maintained, Nicola noted as they drew up at the porticoed entrance, in the most immaculate condition, its paintwork pristine white and gleaming. And the gardens surrounding the house, on which precious water had clearly been spared without stint, were larger and lusher even than those at Garth's place.

There was one other car there already—Garth's, she thought with a fresh surge of panic.

A maid opened the door to them, but in a moment Zoe was coming across the lofty columned hallway, her slender arms outstretched in welcome.

"Nicola! Tony!" she greeted them effusively. "It's so sweet of you to spare the time to dine with us when I expect you'd so much prefer to be alone together."

"It was very kind of you to invite us," said Tony rather stiffly.

"Come right on in," she said. "Daddy's just dying to meet you, Nicola . . . he's longing to see the charming girlfriend Tony has found for himself."

She led the way, floating gracefully ahead of them in the most gorgeous chiffon gown in soft shades of purple and mauve that looked marvelous with her red hair—a new dress she had bought on her trip to Sydney? Nicola wondered. She herself, because of the limitations of flight baggage, had brought only one dress suitable for evening wear, the same one she had worn at Garth's party. Anyway, she reminded herself sourly, even if she'd brought her entire wardrobe with her she still couldn't have competed with Zoe, who possessed a fabulous figure allied to a superb dress sense—which she was able to pamper with the very best that money could buy.

The instant Nicola entered the elegant drawing room she felt the full impact of Garth's steely gaze, which seemed to chisel through her. He stood chatting with their host by the tall, west-facing windows, through which the last dazzling rays of the evening sun were filtered by venetian blinds. Once tall, Howard Drysdale was bent now and walked forward to greet them leaning on a cane, limping heavily. Even so, there was an air of distinction about him.

"Ah, my neighbor and his young lady. Welcome to you both."

"Good evening, sir," said Tony diffidently.

"A drink?" he invited. "Garth, my dear fellow, will you do the honors for me?"

"Certainly. You'll have a white wine, I think, Nicola."

It was a flat statement, not a question. Nicola bristled at his arrogant assumption of knowing better than she herself what she wanted to drink. To hit back at him, she said coolly, "Thank you, but I'd prefer to have sherry. A dry one."

Garth shrugged. "And you, Tony?"

"I'd like a beer, if that's okay."

It turned out that beer was something the Drysdales didn't normally keep in the drawing room, and would need to be fetched from the kitchen—which was done despite Tony's anxious protests that it really didn't matter and that any other drink would do just fine. Nicola's heart bled for him. But she felt irritated, too. Why in the name of goodness did he have to be so humble and ingratiating to these people who in reality were his enemies? Why couldn't he have conveyed instead a certain degree of criticism that in a hot and dusty region like the outback, where a guest might reasonably expect to be offered something as thirst-slaking as an iced beer, none was readily available?

When they were finally all fixed up with drinks, the conversation turned to the weather.

"There's rain on the way at last," Mr. Drysdale predicted confidently. "A good summer wet is just what we could do with at the moment."

"I thought I heard a rumble of thunder today," put in Nicola.

"You'll hear plenty more of that," said Garth dryly. "A good storm here can be quite spectacular. Isn't that so, Zoe?"

She made a little shiver of distaste. "There's something a bit too primitive about an outback storm for my liking."

"Some aboriginal tribes," Garth went on, as if casually, "have the quaint idea that when a thunderstorm comes—a force of nature which they cannot understand—the thing to do is to make a loud noise back in the hope that the storm will turn tail and run." His eyes suddenly switched to Nicola, and once again she felt stabbed through by his intent gaze, which was sharpened by mockery. "As a defense against elemental forces," he added lightly, "shouting back is singularly unsuccessful."

What exactly was his barb this time? Nicola wondered wretchedly. Was he putting himself on a par with the storm? Telling her that fighting against him would do no good? Well, she would just see about that!

Zoe's father had switched the conversation to a discussion of the current state of the wool market. "You must find things particularly difficult these days," he suggested to Tony, "considering what a small station yours is."

"Oh, yes!" he readily agreed. "And my problems seem to get worse each month that goes by, instead of better."

Don't play into their hands, Tony! Nicola tried to force the message across to him, but without effect. He appeared to be almost flattered that the elderly landowner should take such an interest in his affairs.

"Tony will make a go of things in the end," she interrupted loudly, when she could bear it no longer. "It only needs sufficient courage and determination . . . and he's got plenty of those qualities. There's no reason at all why Dandaraga shouldn't become a flourishing sheep station again, in its own modest way."

Howard Drysdale turned to look at her in surprise. "Am I to understand that you and Tony intend to remain at Dandaraga? I was under the impression . . ."

Too late, Nicola realized that in her anxiety to fight Tony's battle for him, she had been digging a hole for herself. "I . . . I wasn't intending to include myself in what I said."

"No?" The old man's perplexity increased. "But aren't you and Tony . . . ?"

"Nothing is definitely settled yet, Mr. Drysdale," Tony mumbled uncomfortably.

"What exactly are we to take that to mean?" It was Garth's voice, sounding bored.

"Well . . ." Tony looked very embarrassed. "The thing is, Nicola's not quite ready to actually commit herself yet."

"Playing hard to get, Nicola?" suggested Zoe, flashing her brightly false smile.

Dear heaven, why had she ever agreed to come here this evening? Nicola asked herself despondently. But since she *was* here, she'd just have to make the best of it and refuse to let them rile her. She faced the lot of them bravely, her chin held high. "At least that's a lot better than being too easy," she said pointedly.

Nobody was amused. Zoe shot her a filthy look, a rush of angry color staining her lovely, ivory-smooth complexion. Tony was looking unhappy and reproachful, while Howard Drysdale clearly was at a loss to grasp the undercurrents of this bewildering conversation.

It was Garth who spoke first, and his voice grated like the rasp of a saw on wood. "So your answer to Zoe's question is in the affirmative?"

"I didn't say that."

"You implied it, though," he said grimly. "The age-old gambit of women—never saying quite what they mean, but keeping everyone guessing."

Zoe managed a tinkling laugh. "For heaven's sake, Garth darling, don't tar all us women with the same brush."

He seemed not to hear her but continued to stare at Nicola. His face was harsh with contempt, his eyes like ice chips on a freezing day. Nicola was dimly aware of Zoe's glance flitting between the two of them, and she could feel the other woman's jealous hatred like a tangible force. The luxurious room, furnished more like a London or Paris salon, began to swim a little before her eyes, and she had to brace her legs to prevent them from trembling.

"Perhaps, Nicola," Garth suggested with dangerous smoothness, "you revealed more than you intended by your ambiguous answer."

Zoe's father cleared his throat and said uneasily, "Don't tease the poor girl, Garth. Can't you see that you're embarrassing her?"

Garth's implacable gaze didn't move from her face. "Well, Nicola? *Am* I embarrassing you?"

Curse him, oh, curse him! she thought wretchedly, and blinked back the tears she could feel welling up in her eyes. Even now, despite everything, she was achingly aware of the sensual ambience of the man. Her pulses thudding, her throat constricted, she somehow managed to inject a semblance of calm into her voice. "Of course I'm not embarrassed, Garth. Why should I be?"

"Why, indeed? It can hardly matter to you what other people think."

"Oh, but you're wrong there . . . it matters a lot. For instance, I care a great deal about your own opinion of me."

"Really?" Behind the derision there was a touch of curiosity.

"Oh, yes," she riposted. "As long as I know that you think the very worst of me, Garth, I know that I'm on the right track. It's your *good* opinion that I fear."

Tony muttered uneasily, "Look here, we're getting a bit personal, aren't we?"

Garth turned and stared at him, as if surprised that he was still there. After a moment his grimly set jaw relaxed, and he said lightly, "Just a little joke, Tony. Isn't that right, Nicola?"

"Of course," she agreed. "What else?"

Somewhere outside, and not too far away, thunder rumbled angrily. To Nicola it seemed that lightning might strike at any instant, right here in the room, the atmosphere was so highly charged with electric tension.

Zoe broke the silence that had fallen upon them. In a shrill, unnatural voice, she said, "Let's go through to dinner now, shall we?"

In the dining room, with darkness falling outside, a huge crystal chandelier shed its glittering light upon the elegantly laid table. Nicola, placed beside Tony, found herself seated directly opposite Garth, so that every time she glanced up she was confronted by his challenging gaze. She felt hardly able to breathe, as if a great weight were pressing down upon her chest—but that was because the air was so close and still, she told herself.

There was another rumble of thunder, nearer this time, and Garth remarked conversationally, "The rain won't be coming any too soon for you, Tony. That borehole we share is showing signs of drying up."

Tony shot him a surprised look, obviously expecting some kind of trap. "Really? The flow seems about the same to me."

Garth nodded. "Too right! That's because I've been diverting a higher proportion of the yield to your side. But if the rain we're expecting doesn't fall after all, then I'll be notifying you that you'll have to make do with less water."

Tony went pale. "I don't see how I can. We've been getting barely enough to manage with as it is."

"It would be a case of necessity," said Garth, with casual, throwaway brutality. "So I advise you to start praying that this storm doesn't pass right over us."

Nicola put in quickly, "Tony, you'll really have to do something about securing your own water supply. You can't be forever at the mercy of a neighbor's . . ." She paused, wondering just how far she dared go.

" 'Generosity' was the word you wanted, I believe," suggested Garth, his blue eyes gleaming with derision.

"I was going to say 'tactics,' " she tossed back.

Roast partridge followed the iced melon they'd been served for starters. As Howard Drysdale helped himself to vegetables, he said abruptly, "Look here, why do we go on beating around the bush like this? I prefer plain speaking myself. You two young people keep talking about the future, with Dandaraga station kept as an independent unit. But even if you could succeed in keeping going, Tony—which frankly I doubt—it would be an awfully hard struggle. So for goodness' sake why don't you accept Garth's offer? It's a generous one, you know, and you'd have a tidy sum of capital to set yourself up in some other kind of venture."

Before Tony could come up with one of his soft answers, Nicola said sharply, "You can't expect to buy a man's birthright with money, Mr. Drysdale. And that's what Dandaraga station is to Tony—his whole life."

Their host turned back to Tony, looking him directly

in the eye. "Is that your own attitude, young man?" he demanded.

This sort of blunt approach clearly made Tony uncomfortable. Flushing slightly, he said, "It's all up to Nicola, really."

"How do you mean?" It was Garth this time, rapping out the question like a bullet from a gun.

Tony shifted nervously in his chair. "Well, I've told her that if . . . if she'll marry me, the decision is hers whether we stay on at Dandaraga and try to make a go of it or sell out and do something completely different."

"So," uttered Garth softly, "everything hangs on Nicola's answer, doesn't it? What power she has in her hands!"

Zoe caught Nicola's eye and passed her a look that was loaded with meaning. But her laugh rippled merrily as she said, "She's almost in a position to name her own price to you for Dandaraga, isn't she, Garth?"

"Perhaps," he agreed absently, still regarding Nicola with his probing gaze. "And perhaps not." With which enigmatic remark he swiftly changed the subject by talking about plans for Christmas.

"I presume that your sister and aunt will be home by then, Tony?" he queried.

"Well, yes, I expect so," Tony replied uncertainly. Nicola knew what he was thinking. Would Angie ever return to life in the outback, now that she'd found herself a boyfriend in the city? Suppose it was just Aunt Janet on her own who came back to Dandaraga, an elderly woman recovering from major surgery. . . . Wouldn't it seem horribly like desertion, Nicola thought unhappily, if shortly afterward she packed her bags and departed for England? Yet what alternative had she? It occurred to her that perhaps in prodding Tony into hanging on to the small sheep station, she was guilty of acting against his best interests.

A moment later she was assuring herself that in allowing such doubts to enter her mind she was aiding and abetting Garth. How he would rejoice if she were to suddenly switch her viewpoint and persuade Tony to sell Dandaraga! With Tony out of the picture, he and the Drysdales would be united by ties of marriage and of business. And Garth Rossiter would suddenly become one of the greatest sheep barons in New South Wales.

When the meal was finished they all adjourned to the drawing room again for coffee. Outside the open windows the night sky flickered constantly with distant lightning, and the thunder sounded like the voice of doom echoing across the lonely bushland. The air was even more close and breathless, and Zoe remarked petulantly that it was high time they got an air-conditioning plant installed, as Garth had done.

"Oh, I'm too old and set in my ways for such newfangled gadgetry," her father objected. "Time enough, my love, when I'm no longer here."

"That will be many years yet," Garth predicted, with a dismissive smile.

Mr. Drysdale shook his head. "I'll tell you this, my boy, I've had about enough of business worries, and I'm looking forward to handing over the responsibility of this station, and retiring. I daresay I shan't quit the outback completely, though; just the smell of the bush country somehow gets into one's bones, and I'd miss it. But I rather fancy taking a smaller, modern house at Alice Springs, or someplace where I can spend my remaining years in greater comfort."

It was all very nice for the rich, thought Nicola bitterly. Everything neatly arranged . . . and Garth and Zoe left in possession here. Would they modernize this huge house and live in it? Or use Garth's super-modern home? Or commute between the two? And fly offf to Sydney whenever Zoe had a whim to visit the hairdresser or go on a clothes-buying spree.

"Do you play, Nicola?" she heard Zoe ask suddenly. Nicola glanced up in surprise to see the other girl gesturing at the beautiful grand piano that stood in its own alcove, seen through an archway of the spacious drawing room.

"Er . . . no, not really," she stammered. "I had lessons for a couple of years when I was at school, but I never seemed to find the time to keep it up. Do you play?"

In reply, Zoe crossed to the piano and lifted the lid. Selecting some sheet music, she rippled an introductory arpeggio, then smilingly signaled Tony to join her.

"You can turn for me," she said. "Garth's quite hopeless; he gets too impatient."

It came as a piercing thrust of pain to Nicola that Zoe was a brilliant pianist in addition to all her many other advantages. She played Chopin's "Minute Waltz" with considerable verve and style, then began on Beethoven's "Moonlight Sonata."

The others all seemed lost in rapt attention. Sick with an indefinable heartache, Nicola wandered out to the veranda, where she found the air marginally cooler . . . at least there was a faint breeze. To escape the lilting sounds of the piano—Zoe's mocking song of triumph, it seemed to her—she slipped quietly through the screen door, down the steps, and strolled a few yards into the blossom-scented garden. How many gallons of precious water did each of these luxuriant trees and shrubs require each day to counteract the fierce evaporation that occurred in this arid climate? she thought furiously. To Tony, that water would have been a godsend, but wealthy people like the Drysdales didn't have to worry about the cost of such luxuries.

She wandered farther. Above her the night sky was densely dark but flickered now and then with reflected lightning. All around her the thunder rumbled, reverberating from distant hills like the threatening sound of battle guns.

And then, suddenly, there was violence and upheaval. A blue-white streak of lightning zigzagged from the sky, terrifyingly near, followed instantly by an explosion of thunder that shook the ground under her feet. Nicola was so badly startled that for a moment she could only stand there, too shaken and bewildered to move. And almost at once the deluge began, a torrent of rain such as she had never known before. She was running furiously now, anxious to reach shelter before she was soaked to the skin. Then she pulled up sharply in confusion, seeing only blackness ahead of her. Surely the house lay this way? She searched wildly all around for the lights, but she could see nothing. Only darkness. With a feeling almost of panic she turned and ran in the opposite direction, until she found she was in a grove of eucalyptus trees.

She halted and took several deep, steadying breaths, making an effort to pull herself together. Rain of this intensity couldn't possibly last for very long, she reasoned, so if she waited where she was, in ten minutes or so she'd be able to see the lie of the land more clearly and make her way back to the house. She could hardly get any wetter than she was already.

Very faintly, above the drumming of the rain on the leaves overhead, she thought she heard her name called out. She strained her ears to listen, then decided it was only wishful thinking.

A few moments later, the call came again. "Nicola . . . for heaven's sake, where are you? Nicola . . . answer me!"

It was Garth! She felt a flood tide of relief and shouted back with all the force of her lungs, "Garth . . . I'm here! Over in the trees! Here . . . !"

It seemed ages before he pinpointed her exact position. He stumbled forward out of the darkness, almost knocking her down; then he grabbed hold of her and held her close.

"You scared me out of my mind," he gasped. "What on earth possessed you to go wandering off like that?"

"I only went out for . . . for some fresh air," she faltered. "The storm came on so suddenly. And then I was scared and started to run, and . . . I couldn't see the lights of the house. . . ."

"No wonder!" he said grimly. "The generator copped it from that first strike of lightning, and the current is off."

"Oh!" she said, feeling very foolish for having panicked.

Garth held his arms more closely about her, as if trying to shield her from the torrential rain. "Never give me a shock like that again," he told her.

Nicola felt blissfully secure and protected in his arms, uncaring that the rain was cascading down on them.

"Why . . . why should you have cared?" she asked in a shaky voice.

"Why? You little fool, this is why!"

With a sudden swift movement he bent and kissed her, his lips cool and wet and passionate. Nicola reveled in their searching, demanding pressure, gloried in his possessive strength, which this time held no hint of brutality. Her flimsy dress was sodden now, clinging tightly to her body, as was Garth's lightweight suit . . . both of them as wet through as if they had fallen fully clothed into a swimming pool. Yet as they stood there in that never-ending kiss, Nicola felt a flaring inner fire that seemed magically to hold at bay the wild fury of the cloudburst.

She clung to Garth without shame or reservation, all her hostility forgotten, swept away by the cleansing violence of the storm. His hands moved over her lingeringly and there was tender reverence in his touch, as if he wanted to cherish in his memory every last curve and secret hollow of her body.

"Oh, Nicola!" he said huskily as he stroked her face with gentle fingertips. And then he was kissing her passionately again, not just on the mouth but on the eyelids, the cheeks, and the chin, his lips making a tingling trail of sensual sweetness down the length of her slender neck to the smooth skin of her bare

139

shoulders and the delicate swell of her breasts. And Nicola exulted in his passionate eagerness, crushing herself with even closer intimacy to the hard, pulsing maleness of his body.

She was conscious of nothing but Garth and her own tumultuous response to him. She could happily acknowledge now that she wanted him, desired him . . . that her body craved for the ultimate fulfillment. It was no longer a hateful and humiliating admission, but something to be gloried in and treasured. She knew with dazed delight that she loved Garth—and it was the most important discovery of her life.

The storm that raged about them, the drenching rain and rumbling thunder, were irrelevant. Irrelevant except that the flashes of lightning now and then granted her a glimpse of his beloved face, the chiseled features glistening with raindrops, his fair hair darkened and shining wetly. And the three people in the house, who must be wondering what had become of them, might have been a million miles away. They didn't matter . . . nothing mattered except this glorious revelation of love.

At long, long last Garth murmured, in a voice that was heavy with reluctance, "We'd better go back inside, darling. You can't stay here like this, wet through and with no protection. You'll catch cold. Come on. . . ."

But Nicola resisted his gentle urging for just a few precious moments more, seeking yet once again the feel of his lips on hers that sent a sweet torment of longing surging through her. Then, tenderly, Garth released himself from the encirclement of her arms and began to lead her through the storm-lashed darkness, holding her close against his side. But when he realized how her flimsy evening sandals were sinking into the sodden ground and causing her to stumble, he stopped and scooped her up into his arms, carrying her as though she weighed no more than a bag of feathers.

With a happy sigh Nicola relaxed against his chest, her arms stealing up around his neck once again.

As they reached the veranda steps lightning flashed once more, illuminating the scene. The drawing room was dimly lit by flickering candles, and at one of the open windows Nicola saw three people looking out. With an exclamation of relief Tony detached himself and came running forward along the veranda.

"Nikki, are you all right? We were so worried, not knowing where you'd got to. I wanted to come and look for you . . . but we had no idea which direction you'd taken or anything."

"Yes, I'm all right," she murmured. "Don't fuss, Tony."

Garth walked past him, wordlessly, past Zoe and her father, and set her down in the middle of the drawing-room carpet, where the water dripped from them both unheeded. Immediately the other three clustered around them, asking questions. Zoe's voice was strident with suspicion, demanding to know precisely what was going on. Garth cut across her impatiently.

"Nicola slipped out for a moment to get some air while you were playing the piano," he explained, "and she was a little way from the house when the lightning knocked out the generator. Seeing nothing but blackness all around her, and not knowing which direction to take, she very sensibly stayed just where she was."

"But what were *you* doing outside, Garth?" persisted Zoe.

"I'd seen Nicola leave, and I was concerned for her safety when the storm broke. Thank heaven she heard me calling and I was able to find her safe and sound."

"You took a long time about it," Zoe said sulkily.

"Yes, didn't I? Now for pity's sake let's stop holding a public inquest and get Nicola warm and dry again. Zoe, will you see to it?"

"Oh, very well," she said ungraciously.

Taking a candlestick and signing for Nicola to take

one too, she led the way from the room and up the wide, curving staircase. As they entered a large and luxurious guest bedroom, Zoe automatically flicked the switch by the door, then cursed when nothing happened.

"I just despise living in these primitive conditions!" she muttered. "Well, you'd better take off those wet clothes, Nicola, and have a hot shower. I'll fetch you something dry to put on. There's a bathroom three doors along, and you'll find towels on the rail."

When Zoe returned ten minutes later, Nicola was back in the bedroom, wrapped in a huge, fluffy pink bath towel. She had a feeling of utter unreality, of being detached from what was happening. She could think only of her wondrous discovery that she loved Garth. She didn't try to think ahead or even allow herself to dream. For the present it was enough just to remember those beautiful moments of closeness outside in the garden in the torrential rain, to cherish the memory of Garth's gentleness and tenderness.

Tossing a handful of garments down on the bed, Zoe said indifferently, "See how these things fit you."

"Thanks."

Zoe paused at the door and glanced back. In the flickering candlelight, her beautiful face was ugly with hatred. "You and Garth were a very long time outside just now," she said meaningfully.

Nicola didn't feel obliged to make any comment. In any case, she wasn't sure that she could really trust her voice.

Lingering at the door, Zoe went on in a tone of ironic inquiry, "I suppose that when he found you, you put on a big act of being scared half to death so that Garth had to console you?"

Clutching the towel more closely about her, Nicola faltered, "I *was* scared. I was afraid that I wouldn't be able to find my way back to the house. Garth was . . . very kind."

"Oh, you don't need to tell me! I saw him playing the

big brave rescuer carrying you back in his strong arms—and you snuggling up to him with your face buried in his neck. How much else of the Tarzan and Jane scene did you act out, I wonder?"

"What . . . what do you mean?"

Zoe took a step toward her, the green eyes gleaming with spite. "Let me give you a lesson about life, little Miss Innocent! There's not a man on this earth who can resist a damsel in distress—but don't run away with the idea that kisses and comforting words at such a time amount to more than a row of beans. Don't go getting ideas about Garth, or you'll come unstuck in a big way. Do I make myself perfectly clear?"

Nicola flinched under this vicious outburst. She tried to tell herself that it was only the voice of jealousy she was hearing, that Zoe's spite was powerless to quench her newfound joy. She clung desperately to her lovely memories of those moments outside in the rain, of Garth kissing her, holding her tenderly in his arms.

Zoe was speaking again, only now she had checked her anger and there was honeyed sweetness in her voice. "Don't forget what I told you," she said, "about Garth being prepared to pay a lot more than he's so far offered Tony for Dandaraga. I promise to give you all the help I can. Look, if you'll persuade Tony to sell, I'll persuade Garth to pay whatever price Tony names. Now, I can't say fairer than that, can I?"

When Nicola made no reply, Zoe went on. "I warn you, though, don't leave things too long, or Tony might be forced to give up through bankruptcy. Tell him he'd better strike a deal with Garth while he's still in a position to bargain."

With that as a parting shot she went out, slamming the door, and Nicola was left alone. She felt terribly frail, somehow, and it was a real effort to draw on the underclothes and slacks and jersey that Zoe had brought her. Everything was a little too large, hanging loosely on her, so she knew she looked something of a mess, especially as her hair was still wet. She dreaded going downstairs, anyway—how could she face Garth again under Zoe's jealous, watchful eyes and Tony's anxious gaze? All she wanted was to be alone with Garth, to have the reassurance of his arms about her once more, his lips on hers sending a sweet tide of delight flooding through her.

She was startled by a knock at the door and called falteringly, "Who . . . who is it?"

"It's Howard Drysdale. May I have a word, Nicola?"

"Yes . . . of course. Please come in, Mr. Drysdale."

He entered, leaning heavily on his cane. "We've been talking—all of us—and we've come to the conclusion that it would be folly for anyone to try to leave this house tonight. The rain shows no sign of abating, and the tracks will be turned into quagmires."

"You mean that Tony and I should stay over?"

"Yes, and Garth, of course. We've got rooms to spare."

"Well . . . thank you, Mr. Drysdale."

"You'll be comfortable enough, I'm sure," he went on, "despite the fact that there's no hope of restoring the lighting until tomorrow. So in view of the fact that you've been through a rather alarming experience, my dear Nicola, we wondered if you would prefer to retire straight to bed, rather than rejoin us downstairs. It was Garth who made the suggestion, actually."

Nicola felt a wave of thankfulness. Garth could understand her feelings about facing him again with all the others present, and he was offering her this tactful way out. "Perhaps that would be best, Mr. Drysdale," she agreed huskily.

"Right! Then I'll send a maid with some night things for you . . . and another candlestick. Would you like something to eat, my dear?"

"Er . . . no, thanks, I'm fine."

"Just a hot drink, perhaps? That will help you to get to sleep." He turned to the door. "Goodnight then, Nicola. And don't worry . . . by morning the storm will be over, and we'll all be giving thanks for the ending of this long drought."

Later, in bed, comforted by the hot milk which had been laced with a measure of brandy, Nicola lay listening to the incessant drumming of the rain against her window. Every now and again thunder muttered from somewhere far off. The sound was soporific, and she soon drifted toward sleep. . . .

By morning the storm was over, just as Mr. Drysdale had prophesied. Nicola was wakened by a shaft of early sunshine that slanted through a gap in the curtains. She roused herself and looked at her watch. Six-fifteen. She went to the window and stood gazing out. The effect of the rain was almost magical. In the gardens all around the homestead everything looked greener, the color of the flowers more vibrant.

Suddenly Zoe's disturbing remarks took their proper place as trivial irrelevancies, born of her jealous spite. Once again Nicola felt gloriously happy. The thought that she would be seeing Garth again very soon made her heart leap with joy.

She felt too excited to remain in bed. Better by far to get dressed and go out into the cool beauty of the morning. But first she would take another shower to freshen herself.

There was no one to be seen as she slipped along to the bathroom, but somewhere behind her she heard a door open and close again quickly. She took her shower, and as she was returning she saw Zoe just emerging from one of the bedrooms across the hall, dressed in a filmy white silk robe. But half out of the door she stood hesitating, glancing back into the room.

"No, I really *must* go now," Nicola heard her say with a soft laugh, "so it's not a bit of use pleading, Garth darling. Whatever would the maids think if they realized that I'd spent the night here with you? See you later on!"

With another smothered laugh Zoe shut the door and turned toward Nicola, who had halted in her tracks, shaken through to the core.

In the first instant of seeing Nicola, Zoe looked taken aback. Then, rallying quickly, she lifted her shoulders in a shrug of indifference at being caught out. But the expresson on her face as she strolled past Nicola was far from indifferent. There was a little secret smile playing about her lips, and her voice was a silky, sultry drawl. "Isn't it an absolutely divine morning, Nicola?"

Sick at heart, Nicola returned to her bedroom, where she threw herself down on the bed in bleak despair. Bitter tears streamed from her eyes and her whole body heaved with violent sobs that threatened to tear her apart.

Chapter Eight

Tony had left Nicola with the task of moving some of the sheep to a less waterlogged pasture while he set off on a complete tour of the property. Earlier this morning, on the journey back from the Drysdales' place—a difficult drive with the dirt road a sea of mud in places, and new-formed streams gushing across it here and there—he'd been anxious in case they found serious storm damage at the homestead. But, mercifully, nothing much was wrong at Dandaraga, though the house roof had leaked and formed puddles on the veranda.

Tony's worried preoccupation had prevented him from noticing Nicola's deep state of unhappiness. And now it was a relief to her to be on her own while she struggled to get a grip on herself. Luckily she didn't need to pay much attention to what she was doing, for the two kelpie dogs did the real work, with hardly more than a word or two of command from her. By mid-morning, though dark clouds still ringed the horizon promising more rain to come, the sun was blazing from a vividly blue sky. The wet earth was rapidly drying out, steamy vapor giving a curious, insubstantial air to the outback landscape.

From out of this tenuous mist she heard the roar of an engine. Then the vehicle came into sight, bucking and heaving across the uneven ground—Garth's Range-Rover! He spotted her at the same instant and

147

changed course in her direction. Totally unprepared for this encounter, Nicola longed for the ground to open up and swallow her.

Garth swerved to a halt, cut the engine, jumped out. "What the devil were you up to," he demanded angrily, "disappearing like that from the Drysdales' this morning without so much as a word?"

Shrinking from the expression on his face, which was as black as the thunderclouds that were gathering menacingly all around, she said weakly, "Tony wanted to get back here as early as possible, to check and make sure everything was okay. He . . . he left a message for Mr. Drysdale, thanking him for his hospitality."

"But you didn't see fit to let *me* know," Garth retorted, scowling. "Don't I count?"

The total unfairness of his attitude enabled Nicola to overcome her timidity. In fact, it served to unleash her own anger. "Is there any reason why you *should* count?" she flared.

Garth looked taken aback by this retort, and his blue eyes narrowed with suspicion. "Plenty of reasons, I'd have thought," he clipped, "after last night."

"Oh, last night!" she said in a dismissive tone, though it cost her a huge effort to sound so indifferent. "You of all people, Garth, can hardly pretend to read any deep meaning into what happened at a moment of . . . of stress."

He looked at her dangerously. "Don't play games with me, Nicola," he warned. "We're a long way past the stage of blow-hot, blow-cold, and you know it."

Standing there with his hands on his hips, towering tall, the sun glinting on the golden highlights in his wind-touseled hair, he looked magnificent—despite the angry scowl on his craggy face. Nicola had to fight hard to resist the blood-stirring magnetism of the man. She felt an almost irresistible impulse to fling herself into his arms, to crush herself against his hard-muscled body, to beg for his kisses and caresses.

If she did not fight she would be lost irredeemably,

she knew that. If Garth should reach out and touch her, all resolution to resist him would be swept away in the familiar rising tide of longing. Even though she knew him to be completely unscrupulous, even though she felt faint and sick with jealousy at the thought of him taking Zoe into his bed last night, to surrender to him ecstatically seemed the sweetest thing in all the world.

Fists clenched, she lifted her chin defiantly. "I can't help it if you choose to place such tremendous significance on what was no more than a trivial, lighthearted incident."

His eyes blazed blue fire, so that Nicola cowered inwardly. "Trivial incident?" he echoed, in a voice of bitter scorn. "You little liar! Last night, even more than when we've kissed before, there was something magnificent about you. For those few minutes you dropped your silly pretenses and revealed yourself for what you really are—a woman of deep feeling and passion."

Her limbs trembled with memory. Her whole body cried out with love for him. In a brave attempt at lightness that took every last ounce of her draining courage, she said laughingly, "You sound almost naïve, Garth. If I wasn't aware of the fact that you've made love to half the girls in the neighborhood, I'd—"

"I'm talking about *you*," he cut across her brusquely. "You and me, Nicola."

She gasped in a quick breath. "What you really mean is that your conceit is so colossal that you expect every woman you so much as glance at to fall down in adoration at your feet." She took another breath, surprising herself by the depth of her fury as she rushed on. "Well, don't expect *me* to provide you with yet another ego trip, Garth. Last night . . . okay, I was rather unnerved by the unexpectedness and violence of the storm. So when you appeared on the scene I went a bit overboard with relief, I suppose. But don't run away with the idea that it was *you*, especially. I . . . I mean, if someone else had happened along in the same circumstances . . ."

"Are you trying to make me believe that you'd have reacted to any other man in the same way you reacted to me?" he ground out savagely.

She evaded a direct answer to that question. "It might easily have been Tony who came to look for me, and not you."

"And if it had been Tony?" demanded Garth, his face like stone.

Nicola felt an overpowering urge to hurt him as he had hurt her—and he had just presented her with the ideal weapon. To have his virility compared unfavorably with that of a man he held in open contempt would be the ultimate wound to Garth. And if it meant telling lies to achieve her object, then so be it; lying had never been used in a juster cause.

"If it *had* been Tony, instead of you," she said, twisting her lips into what she hoped was an ironic smile, "we would hardly have needed to stand out there in the discomfort of drenching rain. He and I don't exactly suffer from lack of opportunity."

Garth's hand shot out and her wrist was gripped by fingers of steel. "So you throw it in my face now, what everyone has been whispering. Tell me, how does Tony rate as a bed partner?"

Nicola's cheeks flamed but she stood her ground stubbornly. "There's no need to be crude."

"Isn't that what you're doing yourself? Not content with brazenly maneuvering yourself into being alone with Tony at Dandaraga, you have to boast about the fact that the two of you are sleeping together."

"I didn't . . ." she began to protest, then stopped. Having chosen this weapon to hurt Garth with, she'd better go through with it. So she amended what she'd been about to say. "I didn't imagine that you, of all people, would be so prudish as to be shocked."

Garth, for once, seemed at a loss for words. She could see the taut muscles of his jaw working as he struggled for self-control. "Just exactly what is going on?" he demanded at length. "Is this some sort of trial marriage routine, to see if you're sexually suited to one another?"

Nicola gave a tremulous laugh. "You needn't be in any doubt on that score," she stated.

"Meaning that Tony is a match for your passionate, sensuous nature?" he gritted. "That takes some believing."

"You may believe what you choose!" She tried to wrench her arm away, but Garth's grip was relentless, his fingers clamped around her wrist so tightly that it was all she could do not to cry out with pain.

"If Tony is such an ideal lover, what are you waiting for?" he demanded cuttingly. "Last night at the Drysdales' you told us that nothing is settled between you yet, and Tony himself confirmed that. So what kind of game are you playing, Nicola?"

"It's not a game," she floundered. "I . . . that is, we haven't agreed to make it public yet, and . . ."

"It's preposterous!" Garth exploded and released his hold on her wrist. "You and Tony Carson . . . it makes no sense at all."

"Tony is . . . a wonderful person," she protested, seeking desperately for the right words to quell Garth's arrogance. "He . . . he's twice the man you are."

She heard the furious hiss of Garth's indrawn breath. "But you haven't tried me yet, have you? Perhaps you should, Nicola, before you commit yourself finally. You don't seem to realize what you're denying yourself. I could teach you a few revealing lessons about your natural instincts that you couldn't shy away from."

Nicola stifled yet another swift leap of longing by giving full rein to her anger. "You have to bring everything down to terms of sex, don't you?" she threw at him accusingly.

"Yes, because that has to be the starting point. If the physical chemistry isn't right between a man and a woman, nothing else will be. Nothing else can be."

Her laugh was forced and brittle. "There speaks the voice of the true philanderer! What you really want is unfettered freedom to indulge in as many casual affairs as you choose without acknowledging the fact that there should be something deeper than sex in a worthwhile relationship."

"And there's something deeper than sex between you and Tony?"

"Of course there is—in ways you could never begin to understand!"

"For instance?" he challenged, his nostrils flaring.

"Well . . . kindness and sincerity . . . and loyalty, things like that."

"For which one should translate—weakness, lack of drive, and his feeble dependence on other people to get him out of trouble," he said with bitter derision.

"That's horribly unfair!" Nicola objected hotly.

"Is it? Try to be honest with yourself, for once. What sort of life is a woman like you—a woman with a deeply passionate nature whose blood runs hot in her veins— going to have with a man like that? Oh, Tony is likable and good-natured, I grant you, but that's about the limit of his virtues. How long would it be before you found life with Tony Carson too dull and unexciting to bear, Nicola?"

She stared at Garth miserably, her throat painfully tight, unable to find words to refute his argument. Because it was true. She was spoiled forever now for the love of any normal, decent man, whether it be Tony or somebody else. She had been robbed of the ability to find happiness through true love by having baser longings awakened within her that cried out for fulfillment. *A woman with a deeply passionate nature whose blood runs hot in her veins!* Yes, it was all too horribly true—and Garth himself had made her that way. How he would gloat if she were so foolish as to admit that to him, much less admit that she loved him. At least she needn't give him cause for such smug satisfaction.

Yet with that devilish perception of his, Garth seemed able to see into her mind and follow her tormented thoughts. He said with cruel sarcasm, "Tell me, Nicola. I want to hear you say it again, so that there can be no possibility of a mistake; tell me again that those minutes outside in the rain last night meant nothing whatever to you."

She said steadily, on a thin thread of breath, "It meant as much to me as it did to you."

"Which was . . . what?"

"It was an interlude, no more. An amusing interlude."

Garth's jaw tightened and his blue eyes glittered. "If that's all it amounted to, Nicola, then why not let us repeat the interlude here and now? If it's such an amusing way of spending a few minutes, why shouldn't we enjoy the pleasure on every occasion that offers?"

"No!" she said, her whole body tensing with panic. "I . . . I wouldn't let myself respond to you, not again."

"Oh, but you're wrong there . . . you *would!* Want me to show you? I predict that your resistance would last about five seconds, if that long."

"What would it prove," she cried wretchedly, "if I did . . . did give way and respond to you?"

"It would prove that my kisses mean a whole lot more to you than just an amusing way of occupying a few odd minutes."

If she didn't manage to hold out against him, Nicola thought desperately, he would destroy her. Destroy her last vestige of self-respect. She said huskily, "I've never denied that you possess the sort of . . . of basic animal magnetism that women inevitably find attractive. But the emotion involved is utterly shallow and trivial, easily dismissed as irrelevant the moment it's over. Think of all the women you've made love to in your time. I doubt if you can even remember their names now."

"Do you want me to give you a list?" he derided. "And I'll tell you this, Nicola, they won't have forgotten me. Nor will you."

She gasped, then flung out her bitterness in a torrent

of words. "Even now, Garth Rossiter, you can still succeed in astonishing me with your incredible arrogance. But get this clear! I feel only shame at the response you can stir in me. Only shame! And if I can't ever manage to forget you completely, the fleeting memories I shall have of you will be tainted with disgust and loathing."

"And Tony Carson is the man whose wonderful personality and electrifying lovemaking will hold memories of me at bay?" Garth's glance withered her with scorn. "Well, Nicola, I wish you joy of him, and him of you. What a combination—a weak, indecisive, fainthearted man allied to a priggish, dishonest woman who is incapable of facing the truth about herself. It's a recipe for disaster!"

With that gibe he strode away to his Range-Rover, leaped aboard, and started the engine. But as he was about to drive off, Tony's Jeep came roaring out of the steaming mist, and Garth waited.

Tony pulled up beside the other vehicle and looked across at Garth inquiringly. "Hallo," he called. "I wasn't expecting to see you today. Nothing's wrong, is it?"

Garth shook his head. "I stayed on at the Drysdales' for a while this morning to get the generator working, and I've just stopped by here on my way home." He gave Tony a hard-as-granite stare. "I hear that congratulations are in order."

Tony looked bewildered and glanced inquiringly at Nicola for explanation. She gave a faint, ambiguous shrug. Then, as Garth revved up and engaged gear, he said loudly and clearly, "Nicola has just been telling me that you two have fixed to get married."

Then he was off in a burst of noise, the wheels of his vehicle spinning on the muddy ground. In a moment he had vanished into the wraiths of mist that curled lazily into the hot noonday air.

Nicola became aware that Tony was staring at her in

amazement. "Is it really true," he queried, "that you told Garth it was all fixed about us getting married?"

"Well . . . no," she faltered unhappily. "Not really. . . . Garth sort of jumped to conclusions."

"But you must have said *something* to make him think that."

When she didn't answer, Tony came and took her hands in his, so incredibly gentle after Garth's harsh grip. "Tell me about it, Nikki."

Standing there before her so adoringly, he seemed to hold out a promise of warmth and comfort, whereas Garth could never offer her anything but brief, fleeting moments of exquisite delight followed by days and weeks and months of torment.

"Oh, Tony . . . !" she sobbed.

In an instant she was in the circle of his arms, and Tony held her reverently, as if she were a piece of fragile china.

"Darling Nikki," he murmured into her dark curls. "Don't be shy. The most wonderful thing that could possibly happen to me would be to marry you. I can hardly believe my good luck. It's really true, is it—you've finally decided to say yes?"

Her eyes were misted as she tried to focus on his face. "Tony, please—you've got to try to understand that I . . ."

She felt his grip around her tighten a little, and he drew her closer and touched his lips to her brow. "I do understand, my darling. I fully appreciate that you don't love me as much as I love you. But that will come. Just give it time, and you'll find that love will blossom. Meanwhile, let's go ahead and get married, and . . ."

Nicola drew back quickly, the warmth between them suddenly turning cold. "But don't you see," she stammered, "it's . . . it's impossible. How *can* I marry you when I don't love you?" She silenced his instant protest with a tiny shake of her head. "Oh, Tony! You must know that I'm terribly fond of you, honestly I am, and I think that you're a very fine person. But marriage . . . !"

"I realize that I've got very little to offer you, Nikki."

"It isn't that!" she insisted vehemently. "You mustn't believe for a moment that such a consideration would count with me if I loved you." She sighed. "If only things were different, and I *could* be in love with you, Tony, I'd think I was the luckiest woman alive."

He said hesitantly, "Is it . . . is it because there's someone else, Nikki?"

"Someone else?" she echoed, taken by surprise.

"Someone you can't help loving, despite yourself?" He hesitated for agonizing moments, then added in a husky whisper, "Such as . . . Garth Rossiter?"

"You know!" she gasped, before she could check herself, and felt all the color drain from her face.

"I suspected it," Tony muttered unhappily. He gave her a sad, anxious look. "But, Nikki, you can't . . . I mean, he's all set to marry Zoe and take over old Drysdale's place."

"Yes," she said tonelessly. "I know all that. I'm under no illusions about the kind of man Garth is, Tony."

"But that doesn't stop you from loving him?"

She nodded wordlessly and stared away across the paddocks. The sheep were bleating and the dogs waited, ears pricked, on the alert for their next instruction.

Tony said eventually, "It's torture, isn't it, loving someone when nothing can ever come of it? I understand well enough, because I've been through the same sort of thing myself, way back."

"You?" She was surprised. "I didn't realize."

He let go of her hands and shrugged. "Guess I've tried to push it out of my mind. It happened in my last year at agricultural college, when Dad died suddenly and I had to quit early to come back and take over the running of Dandaraga. You see, Angie and Aunt Janet depended on me."

"And there was a girl at the college you were in love with?" Nicola prompted.

Tony nodded. "Yes. Her name was Linda. We weren't formally engaged, but we knew right enough that we wanted to get married. But Linda hated the idea of living in the outback. She'd visited here once during one of the vacations, and although she quite enjoyed the holiday, she said she could never stand the remoteness of it for long. At the time it didn't seem to matter much, her feeling that way, because I was perfectly prepared to take a job nearer the city." He made a helpless gesture with his hands. "But then, as things turned out . . ."

"Didn't she understand?" asked Nicola. "I mean, when she saw you had no alternative, Tony, wasn't she prepared to come and settle here after all?"

He shook his head, and there was the pathetic lost look about him of the vulnerable young man he must have been in those days, faced with a choice between duty to his family and the wishes of the girl he loved. A choice, Nicola thought pityingly, that should never have been forced upon him. If that girl Linda had truly loved Tony, she would willingly have made the sacrifice and joined him at Dandaraga. To share the life of the man you love, be with him through good times and bad, must surely be the greatest joy and happiness for any woman. Unless, she amended wretchedly, the man you happen to love is arrogant beyond bearing, reveling in his dominance over the female sex, and without scruple in his relentless pursuit of sensual pleasure. Then there can be no happiness for the woman at all, whether with him or away from him.

"Perhaps," she suggested consolingly, "it's all worked out for the best, Tony. I mean, if Linda really couldn't have been happy here, you would have been made miserable too in the end."

"If I had *you*, I'd never be miserable again," he said coaxingly. "Oh, Nikki . . . please say that you'll marry me."

She felt desperately torn, hating the idea of hurting him when he had already been hurt before, yet . . .

Anticipating her refusal, Tony pressed his fingers to her lips. "No, don't say anything at all. You have it in your hands to make me a very happy man, Nikki, and given time I'm sure I could make you forget all about Garth. Just don't say no, that's all I ask. Eventually you'll give me the answer I long for . . . the only answer I can ever accept. I love you very much, Nikki darling."

Nicola knew that she should tell him right here and now that it could never be. Any kind of vacillation was only weakness on her part. And yet, stemming perhaps from the pity she felt in her heart, there came the thought that if she could never find happiness herself, at least it was in her power to bring happiness to someone else. Whether she stayed here in Australia or returned to England, the memory of Garth Rossiter would haunt and torment her forevermore.

If she became Tony's wife, her life would be rich in affection and mutual respect, even if not, on her side, actual love. How infinitely better a basis for a wedded partnership that was than the crude, calculating self-interest that was motivating the union of Garth and Zoe.

Unnoticed by either of them, the storm clouds had been gathering right overhead. First awareness came with a roll of thunder that reverberated all around them, and Nicola realized that the sun had vanished and the air was close and breathless. Then the first penny-sized drops of rain began to fall.

Tony abruptly came to life. "You'd better take the Jeep back to the homestead before it really starts to pour," he said. "I'll finish off the job of getting these sheep moved."

Nicola hesitated. "But you'll get soaked to the skin, Tony."

The look he turned on her was so full of love and

adoration that she felt a little shiver of dismay run through her. Despairingly, she realized that by remaining silent she had already committed herself in Tony's mind.

'I shan't let a little thing like getting wet bother me," he said cheerfully. "Oh, Nikki . . . isn't life really great when you're happy?"

She gave a nervous laugh. "You don't have to treat me as though I were frail and fragile, Tony. I'll stay and help you with the sheep, and that way we can both go back in the Jeep together."

"Oh, Nikki, you're a super girl! You really are. It's no wonder that I love you so much."

The stormy spell was over all too soon—too soon to adequately replenish the dried-up creeks after so long a period of drought. But even so, the landscape bore grateful witness to the rain in the form of an unfamiliar greenness, with fresh spears of grass thrusting through and whole paddocks carpeted in wild flowers in myraid shades of yellow and pink and purple.

The following days were a strange and uncertain interlude for Nicola. Tony seemed to accept the fact that she wasn't yet ready to talk of future plans. She knew, though, that he was regarding their marriage as a foregone conclusion and that she would soon have to tell him he was mistaken. But she shrank from the task, and meanwhile he seemed to radiate a new zest for life, humming happily to himself as he went about his work around the sheep station.

Only once did he make any attempt to move toward real intimacy. They were sitting one evening after supper, listening as best they could through frequent bursts of static to a pop concert on the radio. Nicola had gathered together a small pile of mending that needed doing, a shirt of Tony's that had ripped at the armholes and some socks that would last a bit longer with darning. For the past half hour she had sensed that

Tony was watching her with a special intensity, and she carefully kept her eyes down as she concentrated on her work.

Presently, he came over and sat on the arm of her chair. He took the mending from her hands and put it aside. "Nikki," he said huskily, "I do love you so much. Can't we . . . can't we . . . ?"

She waited, her heart beating fast. She had allowed him to kiss her now and then, gentle, undemanding, goodnight pecks. But this time, she knew, it would be different. As Tony's arm slid around her she could feel the tension in his body, and she realized that this was a turning point. If he started to kiss her now, it would be as her lover. And if she let that happen there could be no going back; the seal would be set upon their union. She was suddenly piercingly aware that she still wasn't ready for such an irrevocable commitment.

"No, Tony . . . please don't," she stammered unhappily. "I . . . I . . ."

"But you can't know what it's like for me," he said in a voice that was hoarse with emotion. "Being with you day after day, wanting you so much, so near and yet so far."

"I think I do know, Tony," she breathed, feeling a little shivery pain of love and longing as a vivid image of Garth flashed into her mind.

"I'm sure, though, that if you tried hard enough, Nikki, you would come to love me," he faltered, breathing unevenly. "But how will it ever happen if you keep me at arm's length all the time?"

Twisting away from him, she hastily stood up, and—unlike Garth—Tony did nothing to prevent her. She could hardly bear to see the hurt, reproachful look in his gentle hazel eyes.

"Please, Tony . . . give me a while longer," she implored. "I hate making you so unhappy, but . . ."

Tony stood up too, his fists clenched into hard balls. "Blast Garth Rossiter!" he exclaimed bitterly. "I wish the wretched man would go hang!"

Blast him, yes, Nicola echoed in her mind. And yet, if it wasn't for Garth, she wouldn't be even this close to agreeing to become Tony's wife. If it wasn't for Garth, she would still be hoping that one day she would find the man whom she could truly love. Garth had destroyed that possibility, destroyed forever the dream of finding blissful fulfillment in a truly happy marriage.

With these painful thoughts hammering in her brain, she said beseechingly, "Oh, Tony, please be patient. Just give me a little more time."

Chapter Nine

A hired car delivered Aunt Janet and Angie home from Broken Hill just a few days before Christmas. They brought with them a huge hamper of goodies for the festival.

"We've got something else to celebrate, too," Angie bubbled excitedly, then announced that she and Barry were now officially engaged. It emerged that they'd got all their plans worked out, even down to the house she and Barry were going to buy, which had a "Granny" annex that would suit Aunt Janet beautifully.

"She's had enough of outback life, poor dear," Angie explained to Nicola when they had the chance of being alone for a quiet chat. "She really enjoyed herself in Broken Hill while she was convalescing, going to coffee klatches and whist parties and so on, and she made quite a number of friends. Er . . . what will you and Tony do . . . will you be staying on at Dandaraga, or can you persuade him to give up and move somewhere nearer a city?"

"Look, Angie, nothing is definitely settled yet between Tony and me," Nicola protested nervously.

"But it's only a matter of time, surely?" Angie lovingly fingered her diamond and amethyst engagement ring. "You're a couple of slowcoaches, I must say! I thought that being left all on your own here together would bring things to a head nicely. We could still make it a double wedding, you know, Nikki. There's still six

162

weeks to go before Barry and I get hitched, so how about it?"

Feeling a curious sense of panic at being pressured like this, Nicola shook her head dumbly.

"You *could* delay things a bit too long," Angie went on in a teasing voice. "I mean, Tony's good-looking and he's not a bad catch for a girl."

"I think he's a fine person," said Nicola sincerely.

"Well, then, so do other girls!" She gave a quick gurgle of laughter. "As a matter of fact, I happened to run into someone in Broken Hill who's been carrying a torch for Tony for quite a few years now."

"Oh, who?" asked Nicola curiously.

Angie laughed again. "I thought that would intrigue you, Nikki. It was a girl he met when he was at agricultural college."

"You mean Linda?"

Angie lifted her eyebrows in surprise. "So you know about her!"

"Well, Tony happened to mention her one day, when he was explaining how he had to come back here to run Dandaraga when your father died."

Angie nodded a little uneasily. "Apparently he and Linda had quite a thing going, but suddenly it broke up. I didn't properly realize at the time, but Linda explained to me how she just couldn't face the idea of living in the outback. I can sympathize . . . I don't rate it all that high myself."

"Does Linda regret her decision now?" Nicola asked, after a tiny pause.

Angie considered this a moment, her head tilted to one side; then she said thoughtfully, "She didn't admit as much, of course, but I honestly believe she does. My guess is that if Tony were to sell up here and propose to Linda again, she'd accept him like a shot. Not that she has any hope of that happening, now that you're in the picture. Linda and I had quite a long chat and she gave me her address in Adelaide; she was in Broken Hill visiting an uncle of hers who was in the hospital. But

I'm not going to mention anything to Tony about meeting her. It would only upset him to no purpose."

They dropped the subject then, but it left Nicola in a deeply thoughtful mood. After supper that evening, Tony suggested that they take a short stroll along the trail. With the moon full it was such a beautiful night, he said coaxingly. Nicola was about to demur, saying that she had things to do, but Angie intervened.

"Yes, off you two go. I'll see to washing the dishes." She added with a meaningful giggle, "Guess Aunt Janet and I got back too soon, eh? We don't want to spoil the party, do we, Auntie?"

There was a chuckle. Aunt Janet was in fine humor now, and it was obvious that having the operation safely behind her was a big weight off her mind.

Outside, it was pure magic. The moon shed its silvery light across the deserted landscape and the air was sweetly fragrant, with a faint breeze bringing a welcome touch of coolness. They strolled for a while, Tony holding her hand, with the two dogs bounding along behind them, sniffing about happily. Then they came to a halt beside the creek.

Tony began slowly, thoughtfully, "I'm really glad for Angie, and for Aunt Janet, too. Only . . ."

"Only it will make life difficult for you," Nicola finished for him.

"Too right it will, as things stand at present. But it needn't, Nikki," he rushed on in a sudden burst of urgency, "if only you'd give me the answer I long to hear. Wouldn't it be great if we could announce our engagement on Christmas Day? We'd have reason then to make it a real celebration." He put a tentative arm around her shoulders. "How . . . how about it, darling?"

In a flash of insight, Nicola realized that her mind was finally and definitely made up now. But not in the way Tony so fervently hoped. She twisted gently from his hold and turned to face him. "Tony, I've got to tell you straight out—the answer must be no."

"You mean you still need more time?" he asked despondently.

"No, I don't mean that. The point is . . . well, I've kept trying to convince myself that a marriage between us could work, but . . ."

"It would, Nikki. I'd make sure that it worked."

She shook her head firmly. "No, it wouldn't, Tony. Please believe me, I'm terribly fond of you, but it isn't love . . . and never could be, I'm afraid," she added gently. "And for me . . . well, I just couldn't marry a man I didn't love. It would be . . . oh, I don't know how to put it—but it would just be totally against everything I've ever believed in."

There was a stunned silence. Then Tony said chokily, "But, Nikki, I thought . . . I was so sure in my mind that . . ."

"I never promised anything," she reminded him in a slightly reproachful voice. "In fact, Tony, I'd much have preferred to refuse your proposal right at the start, only you begged me not to."

"I know," he admitted miserably. "Oh, Nikki, what's happened to make you so definite now? Is it still Garth?"

"I never want to set eyes on Garth again!" she insisted vehemently. "Never, never! I . . . I think the best thing for me, Tony, is to return to England as soon as possible."

"I don't know what I'll do without you, Nikki," he said in a sorrowful tone.

"You'll forget me, given time. And as for Dandaraga . . . look, Tony, why don't you sell up and go away and do something else? Oh, I know it's hateful to hand victory to Garth on a plate, but there comes a time when you have to admit defeat—in your own best interests."

He nodded gloomily. "But where would I go? Without you, there doesn't seem much point in anything."

'I remember Garth saying once that you'd be much

happier running a market garden somewhere. He mentioned a district near Adelaide."

"On the Gawler River?" queried Tony, and it seemed to Nicola that there was a wistful note in his voice.

"That's right." Nicola hesitated, then said in a breathless little rush, "And, Tony . . . maybe you wouldn't need to be on your own, after all. Angie was telling me this afternoon that she ran into that ex-girlfriend of yours, Linda, in Broken Hill."

"Linda! How on earth did that happen?"

Nicola explained the circumstances briefly and went on. "Linda still isn't married, Tony, so . . . well, why don't you go and seek her out?"

"But I don't see how I could," he objected. "I mean, not after knowing you, Nikki."

"Of course you could. You loved her very much way back, and I'm sure that kind of deep love never dies. There'd be no harm done in just looking her up, would there? At the same time, you could find out what market gardens are up for sale."

"Always assuming that I want to," he said, but there was no mistaking the spark of interest in his voice.

Nicola pressed on while she had the chance. "If I were you," she urged him, "I'd make plans to go down to Adelaide right after Christmas. That way, you could leave Angie in charge here. She'd be able to manage without you for a few days."

"It might be quite an idea," he acknowledged. "But, Nikki . . . won't you please reconsider . . . ?" He reached out an imploring hand to her, but she stepped back, shaking her head firmly.

"No, Tony; I mean it. It was wrong of me ever to delay giving you a definite answer, I realize that now; because there was only one possible answer I could ever give you. So please don't ask me again."

He accepted her rejection in a better spirit than Nicola had dared hope. It was clear that her suggestions had fired his imagination, and the twin ideas of looking around for a smallholding and of seeking Linda out again were buoying him up.

Precisely what Tony told his sister and his aunt after this conversation Nicola didn't know. It was clear, though, that they accepted that he and Nicola were not going to make a match of it after all. They talked about his forthcoming trip—though without mentioning Linda—and Aunt Janet seemed to accept with equanimity the prospect of Tony's selling Dandaraga station to Garth. Now that her health was so much improved, a great deal of her former bitterness against the Rossiter family seemed to have left her.

The thing that worried Nicola most at the moment was the looming threat of Christmas. She remembered with a shiver the talk about all the social activities that went on, the parties and picnics and barbecues. If she was still here, it would inevitably mean coming face to face with Garth on most of these occasions. After one particularly long sleepless night, she suddenly announced over breakfast that she intended to take her leave of them immediately.

The three Carsons were shocked and dismayed. Angie protested vociferously, bewailing the fact that if Nicola left at once she would have no chance of meeting Barry, who was coming to Dandaraga for a few days in January.

"I did so want you to know each other," she said reproachfully. "Please don't go, Nikki. You can't pretend there's any urgent reason for rushing back to England, can you?"

In the end, Nicola reluctantly allowed herself to be persuaded. It seemed churlish to refuse the pressing pleas of these people who had shown her nothing but kindness and affection. But, even resigned to the heartache involved in meeting Garth, it was a big shock to learn that the very first get-together of the season was a Christmas Eve party at Kuranda.

"But there was a party there not long ago," she gasped in horror.

"I know, but that was just coincidence," Angie explained. "The Christmas Eve do has been a fixed event for years now. It started ages ago when Garth's parents were first married, and since they died he's kept it up. Nobody would think of missing Kuranda on Christmas Eve."

"I can't go," Nicola declared. "You all go without me, and I'll stay home."

There was a chorus of protests at this, but even so Nicola would have remained adamant had not the thought wormed into her mind that by ostentatiously staying away from his party she would be handing a kind of victory to Garth. It would be an admission of his power over her. After all, she thought defiantly, there would be a lot of other people present—and this time she would make darned sure to avoid being maneuvered into a position where she and Garth were alone together.

She made one stipulation, however. Catching Tony on his own in the engine shed, she began nervously. "Look, I've got a favor to ask. . . . I'd rather you didn't say anything about you and me outside the family. I mean, the fact that we aren't going to get married after all. Not just for the present."

He looked at her in puzzlement. "I don't understand, Nikki."

"I'd prefer it if Garth didn't know," she explained, color rising to her cheeks. "If possible, not until after I've left Australia."

Tony gave her a pitying glance. "You still feel the same about him, then?"

"I still hate and despise him utterly, if that's what you mean," she stated fiercely. Tony opened his mouth, on the point of saying something more, but decided to hold his peace.

"Mind you, though," he said, after a moment's uneasy silence, "I've got to admit that the last offer Garth made me for Dandaraga is a good one. A lot more than he'd have to fork out if he hung on and waited until I just went bust—as I almost certainly would have done in the end."

"Whatever Garth pays you," Nicola retorted bitterly, "I bet it would be worth ten times that much to him to get his hands on your land. You don't make a fortune out of any kind of business enterprise by being softhearted."

"No, I suppose you're right," Tony agreed, slanting her an odd look.

Nicola gave long and agonized thought to what she should wear for the party. Certainly not, she thought with a shudder, the pink dress she'd worn on the two previous occasions, even though it had suffered no harm from its drenching in the thunderstorm. No, this time she would go in the least partylike garment she could get away with without provoking comment. Her wardrobe wasn't very large, and in the end she decided on a simply cut cotton dress in a soft shade of green that swung rather prettily about her legs as she walked. She knotted a chiffon scarf around her waist as a sash.

When they set out, Nicola did her best to match the high spirits of the others, with little success. Each jolt of the ancient utility truck was like a painful nudge reminding her of the ordeal that lay ahead. When they finally reached Kuranda it turned out that there was an even bigger crowd than before, with the addition of a number of the younger generation who had come home to spend the Christmas vacation with their parents. The garden was turned into a fairyland with colored lights strung from the trees, and people were milling around a barbecue.

Garth, as host, greeted the party from Dandaraga affably enough, though Nicola could read smoldering scorn in his blue eyes when he turned them her way. On this hot evening he was jacketless, wearing a crisp white shirt with a green tie. With his lean, muscular physique and sun-bronzed skin he looked a superb specimen of manhood, and Nicola felt an almost unbearable stab of pain in her heart.

Mercifully, before she could brood too much, she found herself greatly in demand. It seemed that a number of the younger men were anxious for the company of the attractive girl from England who was a recent newcomer to outback society. She made up her mind to enjoy herself, and before long she decided that perhaps, after all, she had nothing to fear from Garth.

Suddenly she caught sight of Zoe, looking a vision of sleek sophistication in a figure-hugging black dress with a halter neckline. Nicola was shocked at the swift surge of jealousy that swept through her like a forest fire. The thought of Zoe and Garth in one another's arms was an agony beyond bearing.

"Hallo there, Nicola," she was greeted in a lazy drawl a few minutes later when the number came to an end and she and Zoe found themselves standing side by side on the dance floor. "Not dancing with your lover-boy tonight? I'd watch it, if I were you, or Tony might slip through your fingers."

"I notice," Nicola retorted cuttingly, "that you've not been dancing with Garth tonight, either."

Zoe lifted her slender shoulders in a shrug. "Garth and I are sure enough of each other not to make a show of our relationship."

Knowing that she was being foolish to tangle with Zoe, Nicola still couldn't resist a taunt. "But then, with you and Garth, it's more in the nature of . . . a business arrangement, isn't it?"

There was a glitter of anger in Zoe's green eyes, but her laugh tinkled like a silver bell. "Whoever it was who said that business and pleasure don't mix was crazy—believe you me! Garth and I are the living proof of it." With which riposte she turned and walked away before Nicola could think up a suitable reply.

As a new number started on the stereo, a pleasant-looking young man with dark hair came up and asked her to dance. But before Nicola could reply, a voice from behind her said abruptly, "Sorry, Jack, but this one's mine."

Nicola froze. Then, as the disappointed young man was turning away, she stammered, "No, don't go. After all, you asked me first."

Hesitating, the young man glanced beyond her shoulder for permission from Garth—and it was not forthcoming.

"On your way, Jack," he advised laconically. The next instant Nicola felt the remembered iron-strong grip, and she was spun around into Garth's arms.

"I . . . I didn't agree to dance with you," she protested faintly.

"Host's privilege," he clipped.

Garth held her close against him, and with only their thin garments between them she could feel the pulsing warmth of his strong body as they moved in time to the sensuous beat of the music. Nicola felt the familiar response to him flooding through her veins, melting away all her hatred and leaving only a sweet ache of longing.

"Well, Nicola, how's the engagement going?" he inquired in a sardonic drawl. "I suppose that having Angie and Mrs. King back must cramp your style somewhat."

"Why should it?"

He chuckled nastily. "My word but you're brazen about anticipating your marriage, I must say! And those two must be very broad-minded. Tell me, do you and Tony actually share a bedroom?"

"Of course we . . ." The emphatic denial dried on her lips. Instead, she forced out a little giggle. "Is that any business of yours?"

Garth's fingers dug cruelly into her flesh. "I dislike pertness in women," he gritted.

"Fortunately," she retorted, "your opinion isn't something that concerns me. To be perfectly frank, I couldn't care less *what* you think."

Without Nicola's really being aware of it, he had

171

danced her away from the fairy lights to a shadowed part of the garden. Garth became suddenly still, and she could feel his whole body tensed with anger.

"Why the devil are you doing this, Nicola?" he demanded.

"Doing what?" she faltered.

"Marrying a man who just isn't a match for you in any of the ways that matter. Do you really intend to go through with it out of some crazy, mixed-up idea of getting your own back on me?"

"I . . . I don't know what you're talking about," she stammered.

"Oh, yes, you damn well do! In the normal way, you'd never have accepted a proposal of marriage from Tony Carson."

"You . . . you're talking utter nonsense," she muttered.

"Am I?" With thumb and forefinger he gripped her chin and forced her head back. "Look at me, Nicola . . . look me straight in the face and tell me that you're in love with Tony."

Those glittering blue eyes of his held her gaze captive. Through the tightness in her throat she managed to say faintly, "Why should I?"

"At least you're not a brazen liar—that's something! Now we're making progress." His cruel grip on her chin relaxed slightly as he went on. "No one could pretend that Tony is a good catch financially . . . so why, Nicola?"

When she didn't answer, he let go of her and said with grim satisfaction, "There can only be one explanation. You're eaten up with anger against me. And you've got it in your mind that you can hurt me by getting engaged to Tony."

She couldn't resist asking, "*Does* it hurt you, Garth?"

His laugh scorned her. "For heaven's sake! If you imagine that I care what you do, you're even more stupid than I thought."

"And if *you* imagine that I'm affected one way or the other by your opinion of me," she tossed back at him bravely, "you're even more arrogant and consumed with conceit than *I* thought. No, Garth, I'm not angry with you. To be angry with someone you've got to feel something important about them in the first place, and I feel nothing for you . . . except contempt. Just let's drop this conversation, shall we? We'll rejoin the others and we needn't say another word to one another, tonight or ever."

She started to move away, but Garth's arm clamped around her shoulder and held her back. Through the thinness of his shirt Nicola could feel his thudding heartbeat. When he spoke his voice was husky, deep in his throat.

"I've got a few more things to say to you before we go back inside," he ground out. "But not here . . . it's too public. So come on!"

"No, I'm not going anywhere with you," she stammered, suddenly afraid.

Garth didn't pause to argue with her but just swept her along willy-nilly. Without screaming and creating an ugly scene, Nicola had no alternative but to go with him. He took her across the yard to one of the outbuildings where a small Land-Rover was standing just inside the open doors. Ignoring her protests, Garth bundled her in from the driver's side and climbed in himself. He didn't let go his firm hold on her until, with a roar and a screech of tires, they raced away into the dark night, leaving the lights of the homestead behind them.

"What . . . what do you think you're doing?" Nicola demanded shakily.

"You'll find out!"

Garth drove hard for several minutes, the Land-Rover bucking wildly on the uneven ground, twisting and turning along a narrow track that was scarcely discernible to Nicola in the headlights, whizzing past scrubby trees and bushes. Then he stopped abruptly, cutting the engine and the lights. Nicola immediately opened her door and jumped out, half expecting Garth to grab hold of her. But he didn't, merely getting out without haste and following her with his long, fluid strides.

In the dense darkness, relieved only by faint star-glow, Nicola peered around her. She could see absolutely nothing beyond a vast emptiness and the ghostly shape of a dead gum tree looming nearby.

"Why have you brought me here?" she asked falteringly.

"To talk!"

"No! I'm going right back," she retorted, and made as if to set out on foot.

Garth's laugh derided her. "A five-mile walk in those shoes across the open bush! You might just about make it—if you knew the right direction!"

Nicola turned around to face him. "Please take me back, Garth," she pleaded, unable to check a tremble in her voice.

"Not until we've had that talk," he said flatly.

"But . . . what is there left for us to talk about?"

"Perhaps 'talk' was the wrong word to use," he agreed. " 'Communicate' might be a better one. What I intend to do is to demonstrate to you the utter craziness of what you're doing by marrying Tony."

Nicola was trembling violently now from head to toe, but she made an effort to keep her voice steady.

"I suppose you mean that I'd have been far more *sensible* to . . . to let you seduce me?"

"I'm only asking you to be honest . . . with yourself as well as with me."

She took a deep, shuddering breath. "Very well, then, I will. I can't deny—and I've admitted this to you before—that you possess a strong, sensual masculinity that has the power to attract women, myself included. But how you can be so conceited as to glory in that fact is beyond my understanding. The way you make use of it is despicable. Any decent woman would despise herself, as well as you, if she let herself succumb to your advances."

"Would you succumb, Nicola," he asked in a tone of soft menace, "if I were to set about seducing you here and now?"

"No!" she exclaimed. "Of course I wouldn't."

"I asked you to be honest, remember."

"I *am* being honest!" she cried, but she knew with dismay that there was an edge of hysteria to her voice.

Garth sighed wearily. "You're being a stupid little hypocrite, and I suppose I'll have to prove it . . ."

"Don't you dare touch me!" she shouted, stepping back from him and feeling a tuft of spiky spinifex grass graze against her calves.

Implacably, Garth reached out and took her in the steely grip of his arms once more. "Want to shout for help?" he offered mockingly. "You won't summon up anything more than a few inquisitive kangaroos, I expect."

Nicola made a frantic attempt to escape from him, but within moments, as his lips came down to claim hers possessively, her struggles weakened, and then subsided altogether. With a low cry that was close to despair, she clung to him wildly, molding her soft flesh against him as she felt his body quicken with desire, her hands coming up to clasp and tighten about his neck. The kiss seemed to spin out to all eternity, the tip of his tongue sweetly probing the secret recesses of her mouth, while each new caressing movement of his hands sent floods of shivering delight through her limbs, evoking in her a rapturous clamor of longing.

The end came with a sudden icy chill of rejection. Garth released her abruptly and stepped back. When he spoke into the throbbing silence she heard the hateful drawl of complacent amusement in his voice. "You see, pommie girl—I was right about you."

For a few terrible, shaming moments, she thought

she might faint. She felt rigid with shock, and had lost all power of speech. Then suddenly words were tumbling out, words charged with bitterness and hatred.

"What have you gained from that little demonstration," she flung at him, "beyond another boost for your incredibly inflated ego? You've made yet another girl your victim, achieved yet another victory to chalk up on your despicable scoreboard."

"That was just for starters. We still have a long way to go before I can chalk you up as a victory," he said meaningfully. "But what more perfect opportunity could there be, the two of us here alone amid this vast emptiness in the fragrant warmth of a midsummer night?"

"You wouldn't dare!" she quavered, edging back from him.

"A dangerous challenge to make to a man," Garth observed with a laugh. "Are you denying that, if I seriously set about it, I could become your lover right here and now?"

To Nicola, treacherously, the thought of finally surrendering to him seemed blissful beyond imagining. She snatched a ragged breath and stammered, "Just because you're so much stronger than me . . ."

"No, it's nothing to do with my superior strength, and you know it. I was the one who ended that kiss just now, remember, not you. And it would be exactly the same if I took you in my arms again—only this time I might not stop. Why not admit that you want me as much as I want you? Why not give in to it, Nicola?"

Feeling desperately vulnerable and at bay, she struggled to summon up the strength to reason with him. "Garth, what's the point of us talking like this? Just take me back to the party, and let's forget about the fact that we happen to find one another physically attractive."

"We shall never be able to forget!" He was silent for a moment, and when he spoke again his tone was subtly different, almost gentle and tender. "Sometimes there's something extra special between a man and a woman, Nicola. Something that burns brightly like an eternal flame, however much they might both try to quench it and fight against their feelings. You want to hate me, yet you can't. You know that's the truth."

"No, no, I loathe and despise you," she cried frantically.

"You don't; you know you don't," Garth insisted, and suddenly his arms locked about her again and his lips claimed hers once more. Nicola felt the familiar rush of delight and longing surging through her body, sapping her resistance; felt the urgent throb of Garth's mounting desire. He was so right—oh, he was so right! For the two of them there was a very special, very magical sort of chemistry. So she would stop fighting and give in, allow herself the exquisite rapture of surrendering to him. With a soft moan she melted even closer against him and responded in a wild ecstasy of passion.

And then, slicing through her golden happiness, came Garth's harsh, mocking laugh . . . not real this time, but echoing from the tattered remnants of her sanity. He probably said the same sort of thing to every girl as part of his routine. With a sudden desperate thrust she pushed herself out of his arms and stepped back.

"Keep away from me!" she ordered in a shrill voice.

"But, Nicola!" he protested, seeming bewildered. "What's wrong?"

She said shakily, "I suddenly remembered what you're really like." Garth started to protest again, but she cut across him. "Oh, yes, I'll admit that you very nearly succeeded; I almost gave in to you then. But what would it have achieved if I had? You might kiss me a thousand times, make love to me again and again—but always afterward I would despise you even more. I've never met a man as despicable and hateful as you, Garth." She took a deep breath and rushed on, "So you can gloat all you like about how you very nearly seduced me . . . and perhaps might actually succeed another time. I don't deny that possibility," she added on a bitter wave of honesty. "But always remember, while you're reveling in your wonderful masculine charisma, that somewhere in the world is a woman who—who considers you the most loathsome creature ever to have been born." With another gulp, she finished, "Now, tell me which way to go and I'll start walking."

There was a hiss of Garth's indrawn breath, and in the faint starlight she could see his eyes glittering with rage. "Get in the wagon, you little fool!" he spat at her. "You needn't worry, I won't molest you. The sooner I can take you back and get you out of my hair, the better I'll be pleased."

He drove back to the homestead like a madman, the Land-Rover lurching wildly from side to side. Nicola clung to her seat desperately, half afraid that in his fury he would plunge off the track and overturn. But she voiced no protest, refusing to speak another word to him, and Garth too remained silent. When they reached the homestead he slid to a halt in the yard, leaped out, and stalked off to the house without a backward glance.

Chapter Ten

All the guests were gathered in the big lounge, where the lights had been dimmed and there was the flicker of candles. Nicola, hovering on the veranda, trying to summon up the courage to go inside, saw them all sitting or squatting around the decorated Christmas tree, while Mary Anstey thumped out carols on the piano for them to sing to. The strains of "While Shepherds Watch" carried her back wistfully to the happy Christmases of her childhood, when both her parents had been alive. Life had seemed so simple in those far-off days. Now, she doubted whether she would ever be able to enjoy the festival again, for it would forever be associated in her mind with Garth Rossiter.

A sudden overwhelming conviction gripped her that she couldn't face these people . . . not only Garth, but all the outback folk who were his neighbors and friends. Impulsively, she hurried along the veranda to the door of the room where the women had left their things and slipped inside. Rummaging in her bag she found her address book, tore out a blank page and scribbled a note for Tony.

Sorry to run out on you like this, but I've just got to get away. At once. I can't explain, but maybe you can guess, and understand. Thanks for all

*your kindness and hospitality, and I hope that
everything turns out just great for you and Angie.
Tell her I'll be writing. And give my best wishes to
Aunt Janet. Love, Nikki. P.S. I'll leave Garth's
Land-Rover at the airstrip.*

It was the best she could manage and it would have to
do. She folded the small sheet of paper and pushed it
into the envelope that had contained her airline ticket,
sealed it, and walked through to the kitchen, where
several wives of the station hands, invited in to help
with the catering, were chattering gaily. Nicola held out
the envelope to one of them whose name she happened
to remember.

"Would you do me a favor, Sadie? Later on, when
Tony Carson is about to leave, please hand him this."
She hesitated, then added, "Or if he should get worried
and start asking questions about where I am before
that, then you'd better give it to him right away."

Taking the envelope, Sadie shot her a curious glance.
"Where are you off to?"

"Oh . . . I've got to return to Dandaraga without
delay, but . . . but I don't want to spoil the party for
Tony and his sister and his aunt. That note explains
everything."

Feeling scared at what she was about to do, Nicola
allowed herself no time for second thoughts but hurried
across the yard to where Garth had left the Land-
Rover. In the circumstances, she felt no compunction
about borrowing it without permission.

The first stage of her panic flight was accomplished
with reasonable ease, for by now she had traveled the
track between Kuranda and the Carson homestead
often enough for it to have become familiar. She had
just one nasty moment, when a dingo shot across the
track just ahead of her and she had to stamp on the
brakes, causing the Land-Rover to skid sideways and
jar sickeningly against the trunk of a wattle tree, which
showered down a rain of golden blossoms. But after a

brief pause to get herself together, she continued on her way. She had to admit, reluctantly, that Garth's vehicle was a lot easier to drive than Tony's ancient Jeep, which jerked at every change of gear.

At Dandaraga, where she was greeted joyfully by the two dogs, she hurried into the house, changed into jeans and a pullover, and started to fling her things into her suitcase. She made a hasty tour of the rooms to gather up the various belongings that she'd left around, and hoped she'd remembered everything. If not, it just couldn't be helped.

On her way out she paused for a moment, glancing around with a lump in her throat. If she had accepted Tony's proposal and they had stayed to fight it out with Garth, this would have been her home. Despite all that had happened, she felt a wrench to be leaving . . . not just Dandaraga but the whole vast region of the Australian outback with its stark, austere beauty. She shook herself briskly. Regrets were useless, a stupid waste of emotion and energy.

Giving Midge and Cracker a last hug, Nicola climbed back into the waiting Land-Rover and drove off. Only now did it strike her that, tomorrow being Christmas Day, there would probably be no flights to Sydney from the local airstrip. She shrugged—no matter, she could stay over at the hotel and take the very first plane out. And once arrived at Sydney, she could make arrangements about her long flight home to England.

Now and then the luminous eyes of some nocturnal animal gleamed from the darkness, and once the headlights picked up a surprised kangaroo. Not having traveled this route since the recent rainfall, she found it all very different with the sudden blossoming of wild flowers and shrubs. Leaving the protection of the vehicle to open and close the gates was an unnerving experience. The knowledge that she was the only human being within many miles of semidesert made her feel terribly small and vulnerable.

At one point, the track divided. Nicola stopped and

thought hard before deciding that it must be the left-hand fork she wanted. But as she pressed on a suspicion wormed into her mind that she had made the wrong choice. Just as she reached the dismaying conclusion that she would have to turn back, the engine faltered and coughed to a stop. Oh, no! She felt a wave of bitter anger against Garth, who had always been so scathing about Tony's not having his vehicles regularly serviced and kept in tip-top condition.

But anger evaporated fast as the full seriousness of her situation dawned on her. Nicola had no real idea where she was, beyond a conviction that she had strayed far off the route where anyone might come looking for her. And why should they look, anyway . . . not until it was discovered, possibly several days hence, that Garth's Land-Rover wasn't awaiting collection at the airstrip? That in fact it had never arrived there! Only then would there be any kind of hue and cry for her. And by that time it might be too late, she thought with a wave of panic.

With pitifully little hope she tried to restart the engine, but it spun again and again without firing. Belatedly, it occurred to her to look at the fuel gauge, and she saw to her shamed dismay that the tank was empty. What madness had possessed her to set off so impulsively without checking that she carried enough gas to get her to her destination?

Sick with misery and fear, Nicola switched off the headlights and climbed out. Her eyes scanned the deserted landscape in all directions, desperately hoping for a glimmer of light from some isolated homestead— but there was nothing. Overhead arched the vast expanse of the sky, pricked with a million stars that spread right down to the horizon on all sides— incredibly beautiful, but looking so empty and lonely to her now. She remembered a tenet of bush law that Angie had once told her: If you break down, never under any circumstances leave your vehicle. It's a bigger target for searchers to find, it offers a certain minimal protection from the blazing heat of the noon-day sun, and, what's more, the water in the radiator can save you from dying of thirst.

The rapidly cooling night air, combined with her fear, was making her shiver violently. She climbed back into the Land-Rover and found some pieces of sacking in the back with which she did her best to cover herself. And so began her long vigil. . . .

Nicola awoke with a start, not from sleep, but from a long, trancelike state in which her agonized thoughts had become mingled into an unknown yearning for what might have been, if only . . . She strained her ears, fully alert now. Wasn't that the sound of a distant engine? A plane? No, some land vehicle, surely? Hardly daring to hope, she reached forward to switch on the lights. As the headlamps blazed, she flicked the switch up and down, up and down, sending out a signal that must be visible for miles.

The welcome sound grew louder . . . or was it only the wild thudding of her heart? Then, twisting around in her seat, still signaling, Nicola saw lights approaching, bucking and lurching, sometimes vanishing for a moment as the approaching vehicle dipped into a hollow, then reappearing again—and always blessedly nearer. Then with a final roar a Range-Rover drew up right alongside, and Garth leaped down. He jerked open the Land-Rover door and lifted her out into the circle of his arms.

"Nicola, thank heaven you're safe! You had me worried sick."

Nicola clung to him in wild relief. "Oh, Garth . . . I was so scared," she gasped. "How . . . how did you find me so quickly?"

"Does it matter?" he grunted. Then, "Well, if you must know, I was looking everywhere for you back at the homestead. . . ."

"You were looking for me, after . . . after what happened?" she whispered incredulously. "But why?"

183

"I wanted to apologize to you."

"Apologize?" she echoed in amazement. "You?"

"Yes. It's not a thing I'm much given to, is it?" he said with a rueful laugh. "But it's the truth, Nicola. I felt an absolute heel for the overbearing way I acted tonight—and all along, too. And when I couldn't find you anywhere, I asked around the staff and Sadie gave me the note you left for Tony. I took it straight to him and demanded to know what it said. So then I told Tony to get back to Dandaraga right away to try and catch you there, while I headed across country to pick up the track to the airstrip."

"But . . . I'm miles off that route," she said dazedly. "I must be; I took the wrong fork way back."

"I know you did, sweetheart, and you've got old Charley to thank for the fact that I found you."

"Old Charley?"

"Too right! If he hadn't taught me a whole bunch of tricks when I was a kid, I'd never have been able to sort out which tracks must be yours from all the other tire marks I came across. But what a little half-wit you were, to take a vehicle off into the blue without checking that the tank was full!"

"I . . . I didn't think," Nicola faltered.

"You don't think about a lot of things, you darling idiot. What on earth possessed you to run away like that?"

Garth had called her sweetheart . . . he had called her darling idiot, with tenderness in his voice. And he was still holding her cradled in his arms as if she were infinitely precious.

'I just couldn't face things any longer," she said in a low voice. "The—the way you always treated me, and everything."

"I know, I've been all kinds of a brute to you," he admitted. "But you made me so devilishly angry. At first you were just a very attractive sheila with whom it would be exciting to have an affair. Only you wouldn't play along—even though it was obvious that you found me attractive, too. I tried to forget you, to tell myself that you didn't matter . . . but I couldn't get you out of my system. You haunted my thoughts day and night. I was determined to win you one way or another, and I set about trying to show you what you were missing by rejecting me. I was so mad at you, there were times when I nearly just took what I wanted despite your protests, knowing that I could give you the most blissful experience of your life. But something always stopped me."

"What stopped you, Garth?" she asked in a husky whisper.

"I didn't know what it was myself, until tonight. Driving here, almost out of my mind with worry about what had happened to you, I realized the truth of what I've really known in my heart all along . . . ever since that day I first saw you at the airstrip. I've been trying to deny it, Nicola darling, because I've always rejected the idea of love—of real feeling—coming into the relationship between a man and a woman. I wanted to believe that it was just a physical thing, like every other time . . . for you, as well as for me. But I'm not fighting any longer, pommie girl, I admit it freely. I love you, I adore you, and I want you with me always."

He bent and put his lips against her hair, and Nicola's whole being sang with delirious joy.

"Dare I hope that you'll be able to forgive me for the cruel things I've said to you?" he asked anxiously. "Is there . . . is there any chance that I can persuade you to stay on, and that one day you'll find it in your heart to love me in return?"

"But I've always loved you, Garth," she burst out impetuously. "Always!"

She heard his quickly indrawn breath. "I thought you hated me? Held me in contempt?"

"Only because I loved you so much," she confessed. "When you . . . you acted the way you did, I felt I couldn't bear it."

"You love me?" Garth queried incredulously. "Oh,

185

my darling, I can hardly believe that I'm so lucky!" His grip on her, so gentle up till now, became suddenly more demanding in his vehemence. "We must get married, immediately. I won't allow any delay, do you hear? We're not leaving this spot until you've said yes."

"I'll marry you, Garth darling, just as soon as ever you like," she breathed happily. Then she went tense as a thought lanced through her like a cold shaft of steel. "But . . . what about Zoe?"

"What about her?"

"Aren't you and she . . . well, more or less engaged?"

"Engaged? Whatever gave you that idea?"

"Zoe did. And Tony and Angie. Everyone thinks so."

"Well, everyone's wrong," said Garth emphatically. "There was never anything that counted between Zoe and me—I merely took what she offered me on a plate. I'm not pretending to have been an angel, my darling, and I guess you realize there have been plenty of other girls besides Zoe. But none of them ever meant anything to me. As for Zoe . . . I'll admit that from the start of our affair I knew she was angling to get her hooks into me. She was bored with being a widow, and I seemed the best prospect around from a financial viewpoint. Besides which, her father had more than once dropped a hint that he'd welcome an amalgamation of his estate with mine, with me taking over the running of the entire outfit. But the idea was a nonstarter as far as I was concerned. Quite apart from the fact that Zoe is just about the last woman I'd choose for a wife—she's much too self-centered and calculating—the Drysdale place and mine put together would be far too cumbersome to handle in the way I consider a sheep station should be managed. I've already got as much land at Kuranda as I can properly keep under my own eyes."

"In that case," said Nicola wonderingly, "why have you been so keen to buy Dandaraga?"

"Dandaraga wouldn't add that much acreage," Garth explained, "and it's such a good little parcel of land that I hate to see it going to waste. The whole trouble is that Tony's heart isn't in sheep farming, but he's too pigheaded to see that. He'd do much better to accept my offer and put the proceeds into something he would enjoy doing instead. Poor old Tony—he's not going to be very happy about losing you to me."

"But, Garth, there's never been anything really serious between us," Nicola told him. "In fact, I've already made it crystal clear to Tony that I can't marry him. How could I, when I'm in love with another man?" Garth went to speak, and she quickly put her fingers to his lips. "Honestly, there was never *anything* between Tony and me. You . . . you didn't really believe there was, did you?"

"At the time I didn't know *what* I believed," Garth admitted. "I was driven nearly mad with jealousy when I thought of you alone in that house with Tony . . . the opportunities the two of you had. And when I accused you of sleeping with him, you didn't deny it."

"Would you really have expected me to rush in and deny it?" she asked. "I mean, considering the circumstances between you and me?"

"I suppose not. And I ought to have realized that you aren't that kind of girl. But when you responded to me so passionately, I had a nightmare picture of you doing the same with other men, including Tony."

"I responded to you like that, Garth, because I love you," she said solemnly.

"I know that now, darling, and I was a blind fool not to realize it before. Mary Anstey was right about you all along."

"Mary? Why, what did she say?"

"She always disapproved of Zoe, as one might expect, and when you appeared on the scene she declared that you were the best thing ever to have happened to me. She told me, more than once, that I'd be all kinds of a fool not to grab you while I had the chance. I reckon Mary must have known, somehow, that you loved me."

"Intuition," Nicola said with a soft laugh. "We women are famous for it."

"Then you didn't show much feminine intuition," he chided gently, "if you imagined I could ever consider marrying a girl like Zoe. I'll tell you this, my darling, I haven't so much as laid a finger on Zoe since I first met you. That's the effect you had on me."

It hit Nicola like a heavy blow that he should lie to her now. She faltered unhappily, "I wish you hadn't said that, Garth, when I know that it isn't true."

"But it *is* true, darling," he insisted.

She shook her head, feeling the sting of tears behind her eyelids. "You see, that time we stayed over at the Drysdales', I saw Zoe coming out of your bedroom at about six-thirty the next morning. I heard what she said to you, Garth, that it wouldn't do for the maids to realize that she'd spent the night with you."

"I see!" he said slowly, thoughtfully. "And did you hear me say anything in reply?"

"Well, no . . . not actually."

"Of course you didn't. You couldn't have—because I wasn't in my room at the time. I was up before sunrise and outside repairing the generator. I'm afraid, my love, that you were deceived by one of Zoe's nasty little tricks. She must have guessed the previous night, when I carried you in from the storm, how we felt about one another, and she was determined to play the spoiler."

"Oh, Garth, I felt so desperately miserable, I just can't tell you. But it doesn't matter now—nothing matters now."

Nicola clung to him lovingly, flooded through with relief. They kissed, and it was a kiss such as she had never known before, the deeply caring kiss of true love which suffused her through and through with joy and wonderment.

Eons of time later she felt Garth stir, and he glanced at the luminous hands of his wristwatch.

"It's long past midnight, darling. Happy Christmas! Now I'm taking you back to Kuranda, and you're going to stay with Mary and Jeff until I get that ring on your finger."

"But what about Tony and Angie?"

"Guess I have a prior claim, eh? We'll call them when we get back and let them know that I've found you safely . . . in more ways than one!" Garth laughed joyfully. "Christmas Day is an especially good time to be happy, I think."

"Christmas Day and every day, for the rest of our lives," she murmured, smiling.

As they kissed again, a dingo somewhere nearby let out a long howl. Far from finding it an eerie sound, Nicola welcomed it as part of the unique pattern of life here in the bush which was to be the backcloth to her happiness.

Abandoning the Land-Rover for collection later, they drove back in the Range-Rover. It was quite a long journey, because twice Garth pulled up suddenly to gather her into his arms and kiss her tenderly and passionately, to hold her to him preciously as if he could hardly bear to let her go.

When at last they reached Kuranda, the eastern sky was delicately flushed with oyster pink, heralding a glorious sunny day.

"We're home, darling," said Garth.

"Home!" she echoed happily, and snuggled closer against his shoulder.

15-Day Free Trial Offer
6 Silhouette Romances

6 Silhouette Romances, free for 15 days! We'll send you 6 new Silhouette Romances to keep for 15 days, absolutely free! If you decide not to keep them, send them back to us. We'll pay the return postage. You pay nothing.

Free Home Delivery. But if you enjoy them as much as we think you will, keep them by paying us the retail price of just $1.50 each. We'll pay all shipping and handling charges. You'll then automatically become a member of the Silhouette Book Club, and will receive 6 more new Silhouette Romances every month and a bill for $9.00. That's the same price you'd pay in the store, but you get the convenience of home delivery.

Read every book we publish. The Silhouette Book Club is the way to make sure you'll be able to receive every new romance we publish.

This offer expires December 31, 1981

Silhouette Book Club, Dept. **SBE17B**
120 Brighton Road, Clifton, NJ 07012

Please send me 6 Silhouette Romances to keep for 15 days, absolutely free. I understand I am not obligated to join the Silhouette Book Club unless I decide to keep them.

NAME_____

ADDRESS_____

CITY_____STATE_____ZIP_____

Silhouette Romance

ROMANCE THE WAY IT USED TO BE... AND COULD BE AGAIN

Contemporary romances for today's women.

Each month, six very special love stories will be yours

from SILHOUETTE.

Look for them wherever books are sold

or order now from the coupon below.

$1.50 each

___ # 1	PAYMENT IN FULL Hampson	___ #25	SHADOW OF LOVE Stanford
___ # 2	SHADOW AND SUN Carroll	___ #26	INNOCENT FIRE Hastings
___ # 3	AFFAIRS OF THE HEART Powers	___ #27	THE DAWN STEALS SOFTLY Hampson
___ # 4	STORMY MASQUERADE Hampson	___ #28	MAN OF THE OUTBACK Hampson
___ # 5	PATH OF DESIRE Goforth	___ #29	RAIN LADY Wildman
___ # 6	GOLDEN TIDE Stanford	___ #30	RETURN ENGAGEMENT Dixon
___ # 7	MIDSUMMER BRIDE Lewis	___ #31	TEMPORARY BRIDE Halldorson
___ # 8	CAPTIVE HEART Beckman	___ #32	GOLDEN LASSO Michaels
___ # 9	WHERE MOUNTAINS WAIT Wilson	___ #33	A DIFFERENT DREAM Vitek
___ #10	BRIDGE OF LOVE Caine	___ #34	THE SPANISH HOUSE John
___ #11	AWAKEN THE HEART Vernon	___ #35	STORM'S END Stanford
___ #12	UNREASONABLE SUMMER Browning	___ #36	BRIDAL TRAP McKay
___ #13	PLAYING FOR KEEPS Hastings	___ #37	THE BEACHCOMBER Beckman
___ #14	RED, RED ROSE Oliver	___ #38	TUMBLED WALL Browning
___ #15	SEA GYPSY Michaels	___ #39	PARADISE ISLAND Sinclair
___ #16	SECOND TOMORROW Hampson	___ #40	WHERE EAGLES NEST Hampson
___ #17	TORMENTING FLAME John	___ #41	THE SANDS OF TIME Owen
___ #18	THE LION'S SHADOW Hunter	___ #42	DESIGN FOR LOVE Powers
___ #19	THE HEART NEVER FORGETS Thornton	___ #43	SURRENDER IN PARADISE Robb
___ #20	ISLAND DESTINY Fulford	___ #44	DESERT FIRE Hastings
___ #21	SPRING FIRES Richards	___ #45	TOO SWIFT THE MORNING Carroll
___ #22	MEXICAN NIGHTS Stephens	___ #46	NO TRESPASSING Stanford
___ #23	BEWITCHING GRACE Edwards	___ #47	SHOWERS OF SUNLIGHT Vitek
___ #24	SUMMER STORM Healy	___ #48	A RACE FOR LOVE Wildman

Silhouette Romance

___ #49 DANCER IN THE SHADOWS Wisdom
___ #50 DUSKY ROSE Scott
___ #51 BRIDE OF THE SUN Hunter
___ #52 MAN WITHOUT A HEART Hampson
___ #53 CHANCE TOMORROW Browning
___ #54 LOUISIANA LADY Beckman
___ #55 WINTER'S HEART Ladame
___ #56 RISING STAR Trent
___ #57 TO TRUST TOMORROW John
___ #58 LONG WINTER'S NIGHT Stanford
___ #59 KISSED BY MOONLIGHT Vernon
___ #60 GREEN PARADISE Hill
___ #61 WHISPER MY NAME Michaels
___ #62 STAND-IN BRIDE Halston
___ #63 SNOWFLAKES IN THE SUN Brent
___ #64 SHADOW OF APOLLO Hampson
___ #65 A TOUCH OF MAGIC Hunter
___ #66 PROMISES FROM THE PAST Vitek
___ #67 ISLAND CONQUEST Hastings

___ #68 THE MARRIAGE BARGAIN Scott
___ #69 WEST OF THE MOON St. George
___ #70 MADE FOR EACH OTHER Afton Bonds
___ #71 A SECOND CHANCE ON LOVE Ripy
___ #72 ANGRY LOVER Beckman
___ #73 WREN OF PARADISE Browning
___ #74 WINTER DREAMS Trent
___ #75 DIVIDE THE WIND Carroll
___ #76 BURNING MEMORIES Hardy
___ #77 SECRET MARRIAGE Cork
___ #78 DOUBLE OR NOTHING Oliver
___ #79 TO START AGAIN Halldorson
___ #80 WONDER AND WILD DESIRE Stephens
___ #81 IRISH THOROUGHBRED Roberts
___ #82 THE HOSTAGE BRIDE Dailey
___ #83 LOVE LEGACY Halston
___ #84 VEIL OF GOLD Vitek
___ #85 OUTBACK SUMMER John
___ #86 THE MOTH AND THE FLAME Adams
___ #87 BEYOND TOMORROW Michaels

SILHOUETTE BOOKS. Department SB/1
1230 Avenue of the Americas
New York, NY 10020

Please send me the books I have checked above. I am enclosing
$_____ (please add 50¢ to cover postage and handling. NYS and
NYC residents please add appropriate sales tax). Send check or
money order—no cash or C.O.D.'s please. Allow six weeks for delivery.

NAME_____

ADDRESS_____

CITY_____STATE/ZIP_____